A CERTAIN
KIND OF
TREASURE

Kellene Despain

GRAY HOUSE
BOOKS

P.O. Box 920142 / Snowbird, Utah 84092

Published by
GRAY HOUSE BOOKS
P.O. Box 920142
Snowbird, Utah 84092

Cover illustration and design by Paul Shiramizu.
Chapter illustrations by Kellene Despain.

Publisher's Cataloging-in-Publication
(*Provided by Quality Books, Inc.*)

Despain, Kellene.
    A certain kind of treasure / Kellene Despain.
    -- 1st ed.
        p. cm.
    SUMMARY: While digging for treasure, two
friends have a fight, which leads one of them into
a mysterious friendship with an old woman from
another world.
    Audience: Ages 9-13.
    LCCN: 00-90798
    ISBN: 0-9679046-0-9

    1. Treasure-trove--Juvenile fiction.
2. Friendship--Juvenile fiction. 3. Human-alien
encounters--Juvenile fiction.   I. Title.

PZ7.D4773Ce 2000   [Fic]
                            QBI00-347

To grandparents and dogs—

some of the best
treasures and best listeners
one will ever find.

Contents

CHAPTER ONE

The Rainstorm

I honestly didn't know what made me walk up the street, around the corner, and into the field on the day I first met the old woman. I mean, I can't remember thinking any particular thoughts that would have led me there. No words ever passed through my mind like, "I think I will visit the field today." When I awoke that morning, it certainly wasn't included in my plans. It seemed like a coincidence, a complete accident.

Knowing what I know now, however, I can say with certainty that it wasn't an accident at all. If the truth must be known, it was anger that brought me there.

I remember how that day began. When I woke up it was raining really hard, so I knew it was bound to be a great day. The harder the rain, the better the day. I know that's not what most people think, but to me, a nice, hard, summer rainstorm is a sign that good things are about to happen.

I was sitting on a chair that I'd dragged over to the window. I wasn't doing much of anything, just watching how the rain looked as it dripped and spattered against different parts of the world outside and wondering when it would stop.

All morning my five-year-old little sister kept trying to squish her way up beside me onto the edge of my chair. Then she kept crowding me, trying to get more room. I tried to ignore her. After all, I knew she was only doing it because she knows I hate it. But before long it started to get on my nerves. Finally, when I could stand it no longer, I sent her sprawling off the edge of the chair. She let out a gasp and made such a weird face when she hit the floor that I just had to laugh. She flew into a rage. I knew what would happen next.

Sure enough, she raced right into the kitchen to tell Mom. I knew I'd get in trouble because she screams louder than I do and always gets to Mom first. It's completely unfair. After all, it's always her fault and I'm the one who ends up getting in trouble. Me, I just try to go peacefully about my own business, but not her. She's always trying to stir something up.

For punishment, Mom separated us to opposite sides of the room, which was fine by me because that's what I'd really wanted all along. I pretended to be unhappy so Mom wouldn't catch on. Somehow, though, I think she knew. But Sassy (which is what everyone calls my sister) was going absolutely crazy. She can't stand to be so far away from me where she can't be in my business. I knew, without even looking, that she was peeking at me over the back of her chair. She was hoping I'd turn my head so she could pull a dumb-looking face at me.

When Mom returned to the kitchen I could hear Sassy slide off the edge of her chair. The floor creaked as she crept towards me. Suddenly, Mom strolled past the kitchen door. Sassy raced back to her seat just in time. I heard her giggle as if she'd just done the most clever thing ever.

Now Sassy isn't one to give up easily. She kept doing the same thing over, and over, and over—always giggling in the same irritating way. Now most people would get tired of it; it would start to get old real fast. But not Sassy. She just goes on, and on, and on . . . forever.

Annoyed, I slid my chair around the corner to a place where I could still see out the window, but where Sassy couldn't see me. I knew this would make her go ballistic. If there's one thing Sassy can't stand it's to be ignored. Bad attention and good attention are both just fine with her, but no attention is unbearable. I could have peeked around the corner to see her reaction, but I didn't, because, to tell you the truth, I really wasn't all that interested.

My attention immediately returned to the rain. Most children don't like rain because it means they can't go outside, but not me—I just love it. I love it because it's the only way to create the perfect conditions for playing a game my friends and I call "Exploring the Nile." It got its name because the Nile was the only river any of us could think of at the time, though the exotic Nile River has little resemblance to the thin stream of muddy water running down the gutter in front of my house.

What the game consists of is this: a rainstorm hits our area sending a torrent of water rushing down the gutter, carrying with it great piles of mud and leaves— and, if you're lucky, something a whole lot better. When the last drop of rain falls, all of us—meaning myself, Mick and JayAnn from next door, and a kid named Bud—meet out at the curb by the gutter. Nobody has to call anybody else or knock on anybody's door. It's an understanding we have. It rains; the "Nile" flows; we meet at the curb, proper tools in hand.

Sharp rocks and twigs were the original tools we used for digging through the soft mud left behind by the "river." Nowadays, however, we're more like the professional archeologists we've seen on TV. Mick and JayAnn bring mini rakes and shovels from their sand pile. Bud's tools are different every time. Sometimes he brings a rusty screwdriver or his Dad's shaving razor. Once Bud even showed up with an old wound-up piece of tin foil. The rest of us never really understood that one. We figured he must have forgotten a tool and had to improvise with whatever he found along the way. Bud's always doing crazy things.

Me, I like to use what I call "The Spatula," which is actually an old paint tool used for spackling. I bent it up at the end so that I can lift up layers of muck one at a time until I see something I like.

We have two rules. First, no one can start until the rest of us arrive. That wouldn't be fair. Second, the first to arrive gets first choice of spots.

As soon as everyone has gathered, someone gives the word and the digging begins. The main purpose is to dig up objects adults would consider too gross to touch. Upon seeing our treasure, our parents always mutter, "That's disgusting!"

Each of us has our own treasure box where we keep our findings. Mine is an old cardboard shoebox. I covered it with brown construction paper and drew a lock on it with a black marker. Pieces of masking tape hold the lid on so it will open and close like a real treasure chest.

JayAnn decorated a fancy hatbox she got from her mom. It has fake flowers glued all over the lid.

The best box by far is Mick's. His dad gave him an old fishing tackle box that he sprayed with gold paint. It has separate slots for each treasure so they don't even touch each other. Of course, the awful smell that floods the area every time he opens it is an obvious drawback.

Bud, on the other hand, just uses an old tomato soup can. It's all smashed in on one side and isn't even decorated—but that's just Bud for you.

Anyway, as I was looking out the window I could tell the rain was starting to slow down and I hoped Mom would come out any minute and tell us we could get off our chairs. I didn't want to be late and keep the others waiting. Once, we had to sit by the curb for almost an hour waiting for Mick to eat his broccoli. By then, the mud was real dry and it just wasn't the same. Besides, I always like to have time to inspect my old treasures first.

I saw Mom glance out the window. She must have noticed the rain was letting up because she gave me an understanding sort of look. Then she told us we could get off our chairs, "but it better not happen again!"

I knew Mom was kidding herself. She knew as well as I that it would happen again, and again—for as long as we had Sassy in our house.

Sassy was smart enough to know right where I was headed, I'll give her that much credit. She immediately rushed down the hall and into my room. Sure enough, by the time I got there she was sprawled out across the floor directly at the side of my bed.

"Move it, Sassy," I said crossly. "Get out of the way!"

"Why?" she answered, doing a terrible job of looking innocent. "All I'm doing is *laying* here."

"You *know* you're in my way," I snarled, feeling my temper rise. Here we go again.

"I'm too tired," she moaned. "I'm just very, very tired is all, and I need to lay down and rest." She pretended to close her eyes, but I could see one eyeball still looking at me out of the corner of her lashes. The sad thing is, she really *does* think I'm that stupid.

"Go be tired in your own room," I grumbled, picking up a foot in each of my hands and dragging her away from my bed. She reached up and grabbed hold of my bedspread as I pulled her away. Great, now the covers would be all over the floor and I'd have to remake my bed.

I gripped her fingers and started to pry them open.

"Okay, okay," she snapped, knowing she was about to lose the battle. "I'll move, but only if you promise to show me your treasure."

Now, I'm the kind of person who prefers to examine my treasures alone, but I figured if it would make Sassy calm down even for a minute it would be worth it. "All right," I said, "but let go. You're wrecking my whole bed."

She rolled to the side and I slid my treasure box out from under the bed. "Now, you must be very quiet and you can't touch anything," I told her sternly.

She nodded quickly, her eyes glowing eagerly.

I began to open the lid, lifting it slowly to add suspense. I took out each object one at a time, replacing it safely back in the box before moving on to the next.

"This one's a feather from a magic silver bird," I whispered dramatically, holding it out gently between two fingers. "Unh unh!" I said snatching it back. "I said NO touching!"

"What does it do?" she asked eagerly. (She asks me this every single time, even though she already knows the answer.)

"It can make people fly," I answered matter-of-factly.

"For real?" she asked hopefully.

"Probably, but I haven't tried it yet." I thought about it for a minute, then added, "And you better never try it because it won't work if you steal it from someone." That, I thought, should prevent a possible future disaster.

"If you ever try it, can I watch?" she asked.

"Maybe." I slipped it back in its place and took out the next one. "Here's a ruby cap that came from a bottle of magic potion."

"What do the letters say?" she questioned. (She asks this every time, too.)

"No deposit," I read, only I uttered the words with a strange accent so they sounded different, more exotic and mystical.

"What does that mean?"

"Those are the magic words you say when you drink the magic potion," I said with disgust. Didn't she ever remember anything?

"Ohhhh," she whispered in awe, her eyes sparkling.

I was about to take out the enchanted rock when I noticed through the window that the rain had stopped. Mick and JayAnn were already standing at the curb. Great, I wouldn't get first choice of spots. Hoping to beat Bud, I slammed the lid shut, snatched up my spatula tool, and ran to the front door.

Mom popped her head around the corner and said, "Going to explore the Nile, I presume?" She knew the routine by now. I just had time to nod at her before slamming the door behind me.

In a few minutes I knew I'd hear the door reopen and Sassy would come plodding out to irritate us. She'd whine for a while and try to make a mess of things—anything for attention. If we ignored her long enough, eventually she'd become bored and trudge back inside to bother Mom.

As I reached the curb I could see Bud running toward me in his awkward sort of way, clutching the tomato soup can in one hand and covering the open end with the other to keep the stuff from spilling out. As usual, a big smile nearly covered his face. As he ran, he raised his hand from the top of the can to wave at me, allowing some of the stuff to fly out, and he had to stop, back up, and stoop down to pick them up. He stuffed the items back into the can with a careless shove and again proceeded on his way with an even bigger grin on his face. We all enjoy "Exploring the Nile," but no one gets into it like Bud does. I think he *lives* for rainy days.

In the meantime, I selected my spot from among many prime locations. It looked like a real nice crop of mud, and I had a strange gut feeling that today I'd find something great. I must admit, however, that I feel that way every time and, more often than not, I don't find anything worth keeping.

Ours is by far the best spot in the whole area for "Exploring the Nile." The street slopes toward our house, topped by a row of fields and empty lots crammed with loose dirt that gets washed along with the water. Sometimes, if it rains extra hard, a pool of water builds up at the bottom. Now and then we pretend it's a lake.

When Bud arrived—huffing, puffing, and all out of air but still grinning—Mick held his hand up like he was holding a starter pistol, glanced over at JayAnn for her nod of approval, then gave the signal for the work to begin.

Tipping my spatula at a sharp angle, I cut a clean line down the center of my patch of mud and divided it into square sections. Carefully, I lifted the first chunk of mud onto the curb and sorted through it layer by layer. I found nothing. I flattened the rest of it out on the cement to make sure I hadn't missed something small.

I'd sifted through most of the squares and was growing more disappointed by the minute when suddenly it happened; I hit the jackpot. In the center of the fifth square was a chunk of green glass.

"Eureka!" I shouted at the top of my lungs. (That's what we're supposed to yell when we make a really big find.) The others quickly gathered around.

"Hey!" Mick said with admiration, "You found the Queen's Emerald!"

JayAnn's eyes flashed with obvious jealousy. "So what," she said. Bud just stared at it and grinned. Then, the three of them went back to their places, inspired to work even harder.

The Queen's Emerald was my only find that day—but what a find! It was definitely the best treasure in my collection. I finished up before the others, so I strolled over to watch them work.

Today, Bud was working with a plastic spoon and a rusty old strainer, which I thought was a pretty clever idea and began to wonder how Mom would react if ours suddenly came up missing. As usual, Bud was really throwing himself into his work. Sweat poured down over a small bruise on his forehead. That's just Bud for you, whatever he does, he goes all out, throws his whole heart and soul into it. I guess that's why he's always getting hurt. Accident-prone, I think they call it. So far, he'd only found a leaf and two small rocks. We don't make a big deal out of those anymore, since they're the most common finds. In fact, it has to be a particularly interesting rock or leaf to be worth keeping.

By the end of the dig, Bud had found a used match "torch," which we decided must have belonged to one of the servants of an Egyptian pharaoh; Mick had unearthed the "mummy" of a dead bug; and JayAnn had located a "magic wand" straw and a chunk of yellow plastic we hadn't been able to name yet. All in all, it had been a decent dig.

After we finish digging we usually take our discoveries over to my garden hose for washing and polishing. I couldn't wait to see how the Queen's Emerald would sparkle after it was scrubbed. There was no point, however, in cleaning up the bug mummy. We knew from experience that Mick's mom would never let it in the house. Instead, we took it out to the driveway to bury it in the garden. Mick offered up a short speech about the insect being from a noble family of ancient bug kings. We all pretended to cry a little as he piled a mound of dirt over the top of it. He and Bud stayed behind to draw some hieroglyphics in the dirt while JayAnn and I wandered over to do the washing.

When we were about twenty feet away from the hose, JayAnn suddenly lurched ahead of me and got to it first. I couldn't believe it; everybody knew it was my day to be first! A sneaky look crept over her face, a sly smirk she was trying hard to hide that told me that she knew too. By the time I caught up to her, she had already turned on the water.

"Hey! It's my day to go first," I said, reaching out to shut it off.

JayAnn slapped my hand away and glared at me. "You're such a big baby," she sneered. "It doesn't matter anyway." She rolled her eyes as if she couldn't believe my stupidity.

Well, I know that words like "it doesn't matter anyway" are always spoken by the one who is in the wrong. I was furious; I possess a strong sense of fairness.

"You're the big fat baby," I shot back, trying to return her glare but knowing I wasn't nearly as good at it. "And this is *my* house and *my* hose and you can't use it ever!"

She darted back and forth, dangling the hose just out of my reach, swaying it back and forth like an angry water-spitting, green cobra—laughing at me each time I tried to grab it. I could feel my face getting hot. "Give it to me!" I shrieked in frustration. "You're just jealous because I got the Queen's Emerald and you didn't!"

That must have hit a sore spot. (JayAnn is an extremely jealous person. She's never happy unless she has the best of everything.) Her jaw muscles clenched and her eyeballs flared. Her grip tightened until her hand turned white. Then she turned the hose on me, sprayed me all over, and finally threw it at me.

I stared down at my wet pants. I was horrified, not to mention completely shocked by the ice-cold water against my skin.

By the time I had regained my senses, JayAnn was already stomping off towards her house. "My mom's gonna kill you!" I screamed after her. "You're going to have to buy me a new pair of pants!"

I don't know why I said it. I knew my mom would never kill anybody. I would have said that my big brother would beat her up like everyone else, but JayAnn knows I don't have one.

13

She turned and stuck her tongue out at me before slamming the screen door of her house. Somehow she always manages to get in the last insult.

I was so furious and out of control I didn't know what to do with myself. How could she treat me like that? I was right and she was wrong! Anybody would have said so. I paced back and forth a few times, then sat down on the steps with my head in my hands.

Trying my best to look miserable, I waited for Mick and Bud to rush over and cheer me up. After a few minutes, I peeked through my fingers to see why they weren't coming. The two of them were still grumbling about how unfair it was that Mick's mom wouldn't let him keep dead bugs. They were busy building a miniature rock pyramid over the burial site. Apparently, somehow they had managed to miss the whole war between JayAnn and me. I sighed and groaned a little louder and made exaggerated efforts to wring out my pants. Still, they never even glanced in my direction.

That was the final insult! If no one was going to comfort me, I'd just leave and they could wonder where I was and worry that I'd died or been kidnapped or something. They'd be sorry they'd treated me so badly when they noticed I was gone.

I stuffed the Queen's Emerald, which was still unwashed, into my box, tucked the whole thing under my arm, and stomped off up the street. A few times, I stopped and looked back to see if they'd come after me, but they were still leaning over the mound of dirt. Some great friends they were! I turned and kept walking, trying to think of a place to go.

Suddenly, a picture of the field up at the end of the street flashed into my mind. I thought over the idea and decided that it seemed like as good a place to go as any, so I continued in that direction.

At the time, I had no idea that this small, seemingly unimportant decision would be the one that would take me directly to the old woman.

CHAPTER TWO

Stranger in the Field

As I trudged towards the field, I remember plotting an elaborate revenge. Just wait 'til next time when it was JayAnn's turn to be first. We'd see what would happen then!

The next moment, I was thinking how I'd probably catch pneumonia from wearing wet pants all day. (I've heard moms warn about that.) Then I'd die and JayAnn would cry and cry and beg for my forgiveness. She'd sit by my grave day after day sobbing into a new pair of jeans my mom would make her buy with her own money. If I did die, I figured I'd haunt her for a while before going to heaven.

I kept walking—and thinking and adding to my plans, not really paying much attention to where I was going—just going for the sake of going. I guess I was trying to burn off steam.

About ten minutes later, I found myself standing in the middle of the field just past the houses on the edge of our neighborhood. I paused for a moment, deciding what to do next. Should I venture across the field and back into the forested area behind, or should I go back home?

I had just made up my mind to veer off in another direction when I heard the sound of a tree branch crackling and snapping over on the far side of the field. Automatically, my head jerked in that direction.

Something was making one of the trees move. I could see its branches barely swaying as though something was brushing up against its trunk. On an ordinary day, I wouldn't have found that to be at all interesting, but at the time I was feeling bored—and, I must confess, a little embarrassed about the fight with JayAnn. So I decided I might as well check it out.

As I got closer to the tree, I could hear a "chunking" noise—for lack of a better word. There it was again, "Chunk . . . chunk . . . chunk."

By now quite curious, I hunched down and crept nearer, crouching behind the bushes until I was close enough to see what was happening.

Peeking through the thick branches, I was instantly disappointed to see that it was just an old woman. She seemed to be working on something. I moved closer, taking up watch behind one of the larger trees so I could observe without being seen.

The woman was squatting down, duck-style, leaning forward, and fiddling with something on the ground. Her back was towards me. On the ground next to her was a large plastic tray holding little cups of dirt, some with little green stems sticking out of them. I decided she must be planting something in the field.

A minute later she reached over and picked up a cup of dirt. I could see her small silver trowel glimmer in the sunlight as she turned her hand. When she set the cup back on the tray, it had something green in it. I realized, then, that instead of placing plants in the ground, she was removing them from the soil and putting them in little pots.

As I watched her work, all bent over, squatting on the ground, something struck me as odd or out of place. My own grandma, who didn't look nearly as old as this woman, could never have worked in such a position. My grandmother couldn't even bend down to pick something up off of the floor. If she dropped something, that's where it stayed until one of us came for a visit. But this old lady seemed perfectly comfortable. Something about the way she sat and the way she moved reminded me of a little kid harvesting seashells on the beach.

Her haggard appearance, however, was anything but child-like. Her hair, thin and gray, was twisted into a tiny bun, pulled back so tightly I wondered if it made her head ache. A few short pieces of hair floated freely at the sides of her face. From where I was standing, I couldn't see her face at all, but her arms were wrinkled and saggy. She wore a pale blue dress printed with tiny yellow flowers, protected by an off-white apron tied in a big sloppy bow at her waist. Underneath, two limp, knee-high nylons hung loosely around the bottoms of her calves, gathering in thick wrinkles just above a pair of plain, brown, worn-out shoes.

It occurred to me that maybe I'd better stick around for a while in case she needed someone to help her get back up. My own grandma has to put her hand on the top of my head just to pry herself out of her favorite chair.

All of a sudden, a scratchy voice broke the silence. "Might as well come over and talk to me. I know you're there," the old woman said, still facing away from me.

Her voice sounded rough and cross. I wondered who she was talking to. My eyes scanned the bushes in front of her, straining to see a face somewhere among the branches and leaves. I saw nothing.

"I said," the crabby voice came again, "you might as well come over. I know you're there. Yes, you, the one hiding behind the tree in the striped shirt with a brown box under your arm."

I looked down at my shirt: striped. My arm still clutched my brown treasure box. She must mean me, but how could she? She hadn't even turned the slightest bit in my direction.

Embarrassed, I stepped awkwardly out from behind the tree into the sunlight. As I did so, the old woman dropped her trowel, brushed her palms on the front of her apron, and popped up from the ground so effortlessly that I almost gasped. I jumped back a bit.

Without the slightest degree of surprise, she turned to face me. Two close-set gray eyes peered out at me between folds of heavy wrinkles. I noticed her nose was slightly hooked and she had a rather skinny chin. She didn't smile at me; she didn't frown, either. Just gave me a straightforward, down-to-business sort of look. I was a little afraid of her. I decided I liked her. I have no idea why.

"Whatcha got there, anyway?" she asked without even introducing herself.

"Just my treasure box," I said.

"You don't say! A treasure box is it? What sort of treasure?" Her voice had a spunky, grandmotherly sound to it.

Stepping a bit closer, I opened the lid so she could see inside, feeling a little embarrassed since adults so rarely see the magic in it.

"Oh, *that* kind of treasure," she said, then added, "the *best* kind of treasure. Where'd you get it from?"

Feeling slightly as if I were on trial, I started to explain as briefly as I could the process involved in "Exploring the Nile." I figured at any minute she'd lose interest, cut me off short, and return to her digging. To my surprise, her gray eyes pierced into mine without even flinching, and she seemed to hang on every word I spoke. If I skipped over something, she'd make me stop, go back, and explain it better. She also appeared to take a strange interest in my friends. When I got to the part about the fight with JayAnn, she made me go back and begin again.

When I finally finished, she stood staring at me for a minute without saying a word. I shifted back and forth uncomfortably from one foot to the other, wondering what was going through her head. I discovered later that her silence meant she was thinking, but, at the time, I wanted to crawl behind something—anything to escape that penetrating gaze. The silence bothered me so much that I frantically searched my brain for something to say. That's when my mind went blank.

At last she opened her mouth and said calmly, "Not good. Not good at all. Let go of it. It will destroy you."

I was stunned. What kind of answer was that? It didn't make any sense. She must be nuts. There was nothing in her answer that matched my story at all. Dumbfounded, I just stood there, speechless, not knowing how to react, wondering if she truly was crazy. I felt the impulse to turn and run or make up an excuse that I had to go home—anything to get away from there.

Meanwhile, she had already turned her back on me and was back down in her squatting position, firmly sinking her trowel into the ground with a "chunking" noise.

It seemed ridiculous to run away from someone who wasn't chasing me, and there was no need to make up an excuse about going home since she'd already gone back to work as if she'd totally forgotten I was there. I think it was the fact that she was so perfectly happy to ignore me that made me decide to stay.

"*What* will destroy me?" I asked, leaning forward to watch her work. She was shoving the point of the trowel into the ground at the base of a little pine tree sapling.

"Anger, of course," was her sharp response.

"What do you mean?"

"Think about it," she replied, working steadily. "You were fighting over a garden hose. A hose! You wasted a perfectly lovely afternoon because of a hose. You may have lost a friend because of a hose."

I felt foolish. She had a strange way of making the whole thing sound ridiculous. But then a jolt of anger flashed through my body.

"But it was my turn to use it first," I said, thinking perhaps she'd overlooked this important fact.

"So," she said curtly, as she gently lifted the tiny tree on the shovel and swung it over to one of the empty pots.

"So, it's not fair," I said.

"Who said anything about it being fair?" A faint smile stretched across her lips. "Are you going to go around evening everything up for everyone? It's a pretty impossible job."

She turned to face me before returning to her work and added, "I didn't say she was *right* or anything like that. But I'm not talking to her right now, I'm talking to you. I'm just asking you, do you want fairness or do you want a friend?"

"But she should apologize to me," I argued. "She even got my new pants all wet."

"Can't make *her* do anything," she answered, her face toward the ground. "Decide what *you're* going to do is all. Besides," she added, looking me up and down, "can't help but notice that your pants are already dry."

I looked down. They were dry—and I didn't have pneumonia. I sighed and felt very disappointed. All my plans for revenge were ruined.

I bent over the woman, watching more closely as she dug out a circle of earth around a new baby tree and slid her fingers tenderly under its roots. Placing it in a pot, she packed more dirt around the edges as though tucking a small child into bed. Giving it an affectionate pat on the head, she then placed it on the tray next to the others. I'm sure it must have been just my imagination, but for a moment I had the impression that the little tree smiled.

The woman turned to the next one. "Chunk, chunk, chunk," went the trowel. "Chunk, chunk, chunk, chunk, chunk . . ."

I waited for her to explain to me what she was doing. When she didn't, I asked, "What are you doing with all those little plants?"

"Digging them up."

"Why?"

"I'm going to move them some place else."

"Oh."

She kept working. I waited for her to say more, but she didn't. I wondered if my being there was bothering her; sometimes my mom said it got on her nerves when I leaned over her shoulder. But the old lady didn't seem irritated. She looked as though she was perfectly happy to mind her own business.

"Would you like me to help?" I asked.

"Would you like to help?"

I nodded.

"Got an extra shovel right there." She pointed. "Do you know what you're doing?"

"I've dug stuff up before," I said, feeling a bit insulted. Did she think I was an idiot?

"That's right, I forgot," she said. "You're a regular archeologist of the Nile."

She handed me the trowel and an empty pot. I found a young sapling and started to dig, prying around its roots with the tip of my trowel.

"Not like that!" she practically shrieked at me, snatching the trowel out of my hands. I was surprised at how quickly she could move. Most old people are really slow.

She slid over next to me. "Are you trying to kill it!? You're missing half the roots!"

"Big deal," I snapped back, feeling hurt. "There's plenty of others all over the place. Doesn't matter anyway."

A horrified look flooded her face. "Doesn't matter!? I'll tell you what it matters! It matters a lot for that particular tree. It matters everything to him!" She tucked the dirt back in around its roots as if trying to soothe it from some terrible ordeal.

I'd never seen anyone get so defensive about a plant before. For that matter, I'd never heard anyone call a tree "him" before, either.

"But it's just a tree," I squeaked in protest.

She gave me a look that was half disgust, half horror. "Yeah, and a person's just a person," she replied. "I suppose you think if you injured one of them it wouldn't matter either. There are plenty of others out there—more than enough, for that matter."

"Of course not," I said. "That would be terrible."

"Well, then," she replied—and I waited for her to say more. But she didn't. I could tell she felt she'd proved her point. I guess she had. I suppose if I were that particular tree it would matter a lot to me, too.

"You've got to do it carefully, like this," she said, gently digging a wide, deep circle around its skinny trunk. "Think 'TREE,'" she added, giving me a quick tap on the head with the end of the trowel before handing it to me. "Now you try."

"I don't want to anymore," I said stubbornly.

She ignored my answer. "Treat it like you would if you found the greatest treasure in that Nile of yours."

She continued to hold the trowel out to me. I didn't take it, so she let it drop at my feet.

"I said I don't want to now," I whined crossly.

"Suit yourself," she said casually. "Didn't ask for your help. You offered." She went back to her work.

I stood stiff and stubborn, eyeing her with secret fascination. Now I liked her even more, maybe because she didn't seem to need me. There was something strong and fiery about her that I admired.

I picked up the trowel and started digging, this time more carefully. Then I remembered my spatula tool and began to use it instead.

A few minutes later I could feel the old woman watching me. Looking up, my eyes met hers for a split second, and I saw a flash of approval flicker across her face. With a little nod of her head, we both went back to our digging. I felt strangely proud of myself; I'd earned her approval.

As I worked, I noticed the soil was still damp from the morning rain. It smelled fresh and rich, just like Mom's plants at home after they've been watered. I paused for a moment, scooped up a handful of soil, and raised it close to my nose.

The old woman must have noticed me pause, for she stopped, tipped her head, and gave me a small crooked smile. To my surprise, she picked up a pinch of the dirt herself, held it close to her own nose, and breathed in deeply.

"Smells real good, doesn't it."

I nodded. I felt more relaxed. The old woman and I were beginning to understand one another.

I don't remember how many little green pines I dug up that day, but I do remember that the longer I worked with them the more I began to feel a connection with them. They were tiny, delicate, helpless. They were completely at my mercy. I knew I could easily crush them if I chose. Maybe that's why I decided to love them instead.

Now and then, as I dug, I'd stop and run my fingers up and down their tiny needles. Unlike the large trees, which were stiff and prickly, the young ones felt soft and moist, almost like sticky feathers. Strange, I'd lived around trees like these all of my life, and I'd never bothered to bend down and touch one of the little ones.

By the time the sun started to go down, hundreds of mini trees were standing on the tray, rows and rows of little children with fuzzy green heads. I was almost sorry to leave them.

I stood and wiped my dirt-covered hands on my jeans. That's the great thing about jeans—they don't show dirt. Stretching my arms outward and craning my neck toward the sky, I noticed that I felt a little stiff from leaning over for so long.

The old woman rose, too. "Got a lot done today," she said, surveying the tray with satisfaction. "You turned out to be a darn good worker."

Compliments always make me feel uncomfortable. I mean, what can you say? "Guess I better get home," I mumbled.

"All right, see you tomorrow," she said as I started to walk off. "Wait," she called after me. "You forgot your treasure."

I had. How funny. Somehow, I'd completely forgotten that the whole day had started with the treasure, the Queen's Emerald, and the argument over the hose. It seemed so ordinary to have spent the day digging up trees with the old woman, yet I'd never done anything like it before. When I had first arrived at the field the treasure and the fight were the only things on my mind; now, upon leaving, they seemed like distant memories.

I picked up the box, tucked it under my arm, and started to run without really knowing why. Maybe it was that the old woman still made me feel a bit uncomfortable. Maybe it was because my legs were stiff from so much squatting. But no, that wasn't it, at least not all of it. Something was leaving me with a strange feeling.

It wasn't until I reached home that it hit me. I remembered some of the old woman's last words: "All right, see you tomorrow."

I thought to myself, "Why did she think I'd be back tomorrow?"

What I should have been wondering was, "How did she *know* I'd be back tomorrow?"

After dinner that night, I went outside and stretched out on the back lawn. I like the feel of grass under my arms and legs—until it starts to get itchy, that is. Looking up at the stars above me, I thought they seemed extra clear, as though they were closer than usual. Maybe they looked that way because of the morning rain.

Staring up at the stars is something I like to do because I know they will always be out there. Lots of things can change, but the stars are one thing you can count on. Even on cloudy nights when I can't see them, I know they're still out there the same as always. For some reason, I can always think better when they're shining on me.

Sometimes, when I'm looking at the stars, my mind will play tricks on me and I'll begin to feel as though I'm floating out towards them. If I concentrate hard enough, I can almost convince myself it's true. I'll start to imagine I'm moving faster and faster into outer space at incredible speeds. Then a noise or something jerks me back to earth, and I'm always disappointed to discover I've only been lying there on the lawn the whole time. Still, it's a funny feeling to pretend I'm traveling into space. I like to imagine it might really happen someday if I just believe hard enough.

Anyway, tonight the stars had their usual calming effect on me. My little problem with JayAnn didn't seem so important anymore compared to all that vast, endless space. Lying there looking up at the stars, I thought about what had happened that day. I pondered over the fight with JayAnn and what the old woman had said to me.

By the time I climbed into bed, I knew exactly what I would do.

never get the ball." Down below there were small, shabby-looking, houses with grubby, weed-infested gardens and yards strewn with old cars. I noticed that the houses in my neighborhood were somewhere in between the two extremes.

Once again, she pointed quickly to the left and said, "The flowers," then to the right and said, "The weeds." She looked me in the eye and added, "The flowers are valued and admired because everything about them appears beautiful. Does that mean the weeds don't have just as much right to exist? Some think so. That's one of the problems with this world."

"Yuck," I said, pointing down to one of the worst houses below. "I'd sure hate to live there." The roof was caving in on one side, a pile of car parts lay rusting in the backyard, and an old toilet rested on the front lawn.

"You don't even know who lives there, do you?" she said.

I shook my head.

"I'll bet you know who lives over there," she said pointing the other way.

"Yep," I answered quickly, "that's the mayor's home."

Without another word, she turned and headed back down the hill.

CHAPTER FOUR

House of Plants

I remained up on the hill a minute longer, gazing down at the houses below. Then I turned and followed after the old lady. By then, she was way ahead of me, so I had plenty of time to think. I thought about how the flowers get all the love, praise, and attention, but everybody hates the weeds. No one thinks they're any good. No one ever treats them like their special. But the weeds can't help it that they're weeds. They'd probably rather be flowers too.

So we spent the rest of the afternoon digging up different kinds of weeds, only this time I treated them with greater respect. After all, who's to say what's a weed and what's a flower?

"Well," the old woman said at last. "With your help I'm getting the work done twice as fast. Let's call it a day. You snatch that tray over there and I'll take this one."

"What about my bike?" I called after her.

"What about it?"

"What should I do with it? I can't ride it if I carry the tray."

"Oh, just leave it here for a while then."

"But someone might steal it."

A puzzled look crossed her face, as if she didn't understand what I could possibly mean. Then it dawned on her. She tipped her head thoughtfully to one side and said, "Oh yes, I forgot. You have to worry about that here, don't you."

Before I could say anything, she charged over to the bike, hopped right on, and rode it over to a thick cluster of bushes. She sure looked silly—an old lady like her riding a kid's bike. I do have to admit, however, that she was quite coordinated. With ease, she hoisted the bike up to her shoulder then stuffed it right into the middle of a thick clump of bushes.

"It'll be there when you get back, I'll guarantee it," she said as she lifted her tray and led the way.

Since I didn't know where we were going, I had no choice but to follow. We trudged across the field until we came to a street on the other side. Then she walked clear to the end, me still lagging behind.

Way off by itself was an ordinary looking white house with a green door and shutters. It was just the type you'd expect a little old lady to live in.

As we moved up the sidewalk towards the front door, my eyes wandered back and forth across the yard, straining to find the spot where she'd planted the little green pine trees. I couldn't see them anywhere. They must be somewhere out back, I decided.

To my surprise, the old woman opened the front door and carried her tray of weeds right into the house. I followed her.

It was an odd looking place. There was hardly any furniture, only a small bed in the corner with a lamp beside it. A tiny kitchen with only a few cupboards and appliances was wedged over on the opposite side. But the room was far from bare: The entire floor of the house was covered with row upon row of trays filled with all kinds of seedlings—including the tiny pines we'd collected the day before. I recognized some of the wild flowers, bushes, and, yes, even weeds I'd seen growing here and there in my neighborhood. What anyone would do with so many plants I couldn't imagine.

"Aren't you ever going to plant any of them?" I asked curiously.

"Oh my, yes," she answered. "Every last one of them will be used. You can depend on that." Then she added, pointing to one of the only empty spots on the floor, "You can set those right over there. Now, I'll get us a snack."

I watched her weave effortlessly through the maze of potted plants towards the kitchen. She took out a carton of orange juice and a package of cookies, then motioned for me to follow her out the back door. I tiptoed as best I could through the maze of plants to the back porch, stopping once or twice to upright a few pots I'd knocked over on the way.

Outside was a little porch with a swing hanging from the roof. We sat down and started in on the cookies and orange juice—two of my favorite snacks.

"My mother would be mad if she knew I was having treats so close to dinner," I said as I crunched down a second cookie.

"Oh, she wouldn't mind if she knew how hard you'd been working," she replied. "Besides, we missed lunch."

It felt really good to collapse on the comfortable old swing after squatting and hunching over all day. I noticed how tired I was, sunburned, too. I also noticed the shadows on the lawn were growing longer and darker.

I lifted my aching body from the swing. "It's getting close to dinner," I said. "I'd better go now."

She peered out at the sinking sun, looked back at me, and nodded.

"Thanks for the food."

She nodded again.

As I was walking away, she called me back.

"Hey," she said, "JayAnn might act as if she won, but she didn't."

It was such a simple thing to say, but it left me with a good feeling inside. I knew at that moment that I'd done a good thing. I strolled back across the field and pulled my bike out of the bushes. She was right. It was still there.

On the way home, I thought about the mayor—which was weird because I never think about stuff like that. I guess it was due to seeing his house from the top of the hill. He was definitely a flower. People always flocked around him, admired him, and did what he said. I'd seen glimpses of him on TV, but, like most kids, I flip the channel as soon as I see it's something political. The worst is when the president is on because you just know he's gonna be on every single station, and the TV night is a total waste. But I'd seen the mayor enough to see him smiling his big happy grin, just like a flower would if it could. I wondered if he was really as happy as he looked. For some reason, I didn't think so.

Then I thought about the president. He always has a huge group of people following him around. Somehow, I don't think I'd like hanging around him too much. He seems so cold and stiff and unreal, not like someone you could sit and talk to and share a bag of popcorn with.

This led me to consider who I would choose for president. Who did I really like? Whose face would I want to see on every TV channel?

Immediately, I thought of Mr. Edgar, the little old man who lives a couple of streets over from us. I see him almost every week because he's always out walking his dog. His pockets are stuffed full of candy for kids he happens to pass. He likes us all. If anyone has an emergency like a flat bike tire that needs air or a frog that needs to be fed, the answer is always, "Let's go ask Mr. Edgar. He'll know what to do." That man is the smartest person I know, and he's never too busy to help. But, best of all, he gives me a pat on the head each time he sees me and never forgets my name.

How would it be to have a president who walks his dog and gives out treats and pats on the head instead of sitting in the White House working on wars and taxes? I tried to picture Mr. Edgar wearing a suit, talking on TV, and living in the White House. I couldn't even imagine it without laughing. He's too different from most politicians—who are more the type that would rip the ball right out of your hands if they could get away with it. But Mr. Edgar, why, if you played a game of ball with him, he'd let you win just to see you smile.

Then it hit me that most adults would probably consider Mr. Edgar a weed because he doesn't dress fancy and lives all alone in a plain little house. But that doesn't matter. The kids in the neighborhood know he's a flower.

"She's right," I thought to myself. "The old lady's right. Some things are all mixed up."

That's okay though, because Mr. Edgar would never want to be president anyway. Maybe that's just the point: if he was the type who wanted to be president, I probably wouldn't want him to be.

When I walked inside the house, Sassy was standing on a chair by the stove "helping" Mom cook. She appeared extra cranky. She was probably upset that I hadn't been around for her to irritate all day.

"Where have you been all day?" Mom asked.

"I headed off for a bike ride and ran into a new friend of mine."

"Sounds fun." (She was only half listening because she was trying to keep Sassy from burning herself on the pan.)

While I was eating dinner, I could see Mick and JayAnn out playing on their front lawn. When we finished, Sassy and I went out to play too. Mom seemed relieved; I think she was tired of trying to entertain Sassy.

When they saw us, Mick waved for us to come over. JayAnn just gave me a sly smile that had a good deal of smugness to it. She looked a little bit too triumphant. Still, I thought about what the old lady had said and felt glad that we were friends again. Things were more peaceful this way.

We had already played Tag and were just finishing up Statue Maker when Bud came to join us. He was limping a little like he must have sprained an ankle, but, as usual, he was grinning from ear to ear.

"What'd you do this time?" Mick teased, jabbing Bud in the side with his elbow. "Twist your ankle again or something?"

Bud just shrugged it off and kept on smiling. We were used to his peculiar injuries by now; there was always something. Mom said an active boy like Bud was bound to have an accident now and then, especially since he's a bit clumsy.

Usually when Mom calls us in for bed I try to stall for more time, but tonight I was dead tired and staggered right inside. Sassy, of course, screamed bloody murder and Mom had to chase her all over the yard, threatening and yelling, before she finally caught her and dragged her up the steps. Then she had to stuff her through the doorway, which was harder than it sounds since Sassy had all of her arms and legs spread out as wide as they could go. Mom received a nasty bite on the arm in the process, but finally managed to wrestle her into the hallway. She heaved Sassy over one shoulder so she could carry her down the hall into her bedroom.

I was so sleepy I could hardly grip my toothbrush. Sassy, on the other hand, had gotten away without brushing her teeth at all. Half way down the hall she had fallen asleep. Just seconds before she'd been screaming, "I'M NOT TIRED!"

Dad took her from Mom and tucked her into bed in her clothes. Nobody wants to risk waking Sassy once she's peacefully asleep. When she's asleep, she looks so different, a lot nicer, even a bit innocent. At those moments, it's hard to believe she's such a terror during daylight hours. I guess she's the opposite of a vampire.

Before climbing into bed, I sat for a moment and looked out my window. My eyes were so tired that everything was blurry. I think I just needed to see the stars before going to sleep.

I think I just wanted to know they were still out there shining down on me.

CHAPTER FIVE

The Meadow

I left to go to the field the next day right after breakfast. Sassy whined and cried, begging to go with me. I told Mom it was too far to take such a little kid. Hearing herself referred to as a "little kid" sent Sassy into a frenzy. Mom had to banish her to her room to cool off. I hadn't meant to get Sassy all frazzled. It's just that, to me, that's what she is, a little kid. As I walked out the door I even felt kind of sorry for her. It's hard to be little and think that you're big.

I was surprised to find the old woman waiting for me, seated on a big rock with her ankles crossed. Resting on the ground next to her were two silver, wire cages. She held two others, one in each hand. I wondered how long she'd been waiting. The last two days I had come to the field much later. Would she have waited for me there on the rock for hours? What if I hadn't come at all?

"Hi," I said as I approached. "Have you been here long?"

"Nope. Just got here," she said, rising to her feet.

It was then I first realized that a strange sort of understanding was growing between us. I kept finding myself drawn to the field, and she was always there to greet me. Once I arrived, she never explained to me what we'd be doing. She'd just start right in, and I'd follow her as though it was the most natural thing in the world. I guess friends sometimes have funny things like that happen to them, like when one of them seems to know what the other is thinking, or when they can finish each other's sentences. I guess it meant we were becoming friends.

She headed toward the back of the field where it meets the forest. I picked up the other two cages, somehow knowing she'd left them for me, and followed a few feet behind her.

Entering the forest, we hiked for about half an hour before reaching a grassy meadow. Immediately, it struck me as strange that I'd lived in the area all of my life, yet I'd never been there before. It wasn't even all that far away from my house. Don't get me wrong, my friends and I had ventured into the forest many times before. Once we were in, however, we didn't go much further, just goofed around and played hide-and-seek. I guess we thought the rest of it would just be more of the same. We were wrong.

The meadow was a magical place, all yellow-green and fresh and completely surrounded by thick trees. A stream twisted through it, wandering at will and occasionally overflowing here and there to form a series of ponds. I thought to myself that in the future I'd be coming here often. I didn't know how right I was.

"This looks like the right place to sit and wait," she said, setting the cages on the ground.

I followed her example, then asked, "What are we waiting for?"

"Rabbits," she said, as if it were the most ordinary thing in the world to sit in a field and wait for rabbits.

So that's what the cages were for. The idea made me feel a bit uneasy. After all, I love animals and wasn't sure I liked the idea of catching wild creatures and putting them in cages. Still, I was curious to see how she would go about catching one, so I kept my mouth sealed shut.

We stayed in the meadow for a really long time. We played in the stream, even took our shoes and socks off and stuck our feet in to cool them. We wandered about, studying plants and strange looking bugs. The whole time I kept my eyes peeled for rabbits, though I thought it strange that she never seemed to be looking for them at all.

The old woman was completely absorbed in whatever we were doing at the moment, except that every now and then she'd sit down to relax. Then she'd close her eyes and squint them tightly as if they hurt. Sometimes she'd rub them a little. I wondered if the glare of the sun and the dryness of the wind were bothering her. Even my young eyes were itching a bit.

Hours had passed and we'd explored most of the meadow. I was getting restless and bored—and I hadn't seen the slightest trace of a rabbit.

"Wouldn't it be better if we went and looked for some?" I suggested at last.

She looked at me as though I were insane for suggesting such a thing. "When they're ready they'll come," was her somewhat sharp answer. "You on a tight time schedule or something?"

"No," I said sheepishly. "I'm just bored."

"Bored!" she said in surprise. "There's plenty to do."

"Like what?" I questioned.

"Like what?!" she shot back, exasperated. "Why, we're out here in the middle of nowhere. If nothing else, simply enjoy the fact that you're somewhere different today."

I thought about her words. I pictured myself back at home with Sassy. Things could definitely be worse. I tried again anyway. "But we've already explored the whole meadow," I said.

She opened her eyes wide, "Then go do it again. Don't you think there might be something you've missed?"

I could tell I'd get no sympathy from her and it made me a little sulky. After all, I was just a kid. Kids have short attention spans. I know, because I've heard adults say so. I had a legitimate reason to be grumpy.

Then I remembered how, just like Sassy, I hate it when adults say I can't do something because I'm a kid. I realized she was treating me just the way I'd always wanted to be treated—like a real person, like an equal. And if that meant giving up some of the special favors of being a child it was worth it. At least she never talked down to me or told me I couldn't do something.

"Or," she continued after a moment, "you can go home if you'd like. You're the one who'll be missing out."

As an answer, I stretched out on the ground next to her. I was staying; there was no way I'd take a chance of missing out on anything.

About fifteen minutes later, she reached down and drew a brown sack out of one of her big apron pockets. I'd seen the top of it sticking out earlier and had wondered what was inside. I had assumed it was bait to trap the rabbits. I was wrong.

Opening it up, the old woman pulled out a plastic thermos of water and two wrapped sandwiches. She handed one of them to me and bit into the other.

"What'd you do when you got home last night?" she asked between bites.

I told her about playing games with my friends outside on the lawn. She nodded her head in approval as I described the fun we'd had.

"That Bud sounds like an interesting boy," she said when I'd finished talking.

I was surprised at her comment. I'd hardly said a word about Bud. And he was far from being "interesting"—rather just the opposite. He was someone who was just sort of there in the background. He kind of showed up one day and kept coming back. No one seemed to mind. I tried to explain this to her. She cut me off in the middle of a sentence.

"I tell you, that Bud is a jewel of the Nile." She spoke the words as though there was no room for doubt or argument.

I stared at the old woman. Sometimes I still thought she was loony. What was she talking about? Bud, a jewel? Accident-prone, clumsy Bud? Sure, he was an okay guy, but a jewel? Then I was surprised to realize, when I thought of him, that I really didn't know all that much about him. But what was there to know, anyway?

Detecting my confusion, she explained, "In the past, when you've walked out to the gutter to 'explore the Nile,' as you call it, what's the first thing you've seen when you looked down?"

I thought for a second, then said, "Mud, I guess."

"That's right," she replied. "Plain, ordinary mud. Well now, if you never bothered to stop and dig around in it, would you ever know there was anything else down below? Would you ever find all that great treasure lying just beneath the surface?"

"No."

"Would that mean that there wasn't anything there, that it was just all mud and nothing else?"

"No."

"Well then, next time you see Bud, look a little closer, dig a little deeper."

I still thought she was wrong. Bud was an ordinary guy and she was just trying to start an argument with me like she always does. How would she know, anyway? She'd never even met him.

I was about to say so, when suddenly her head popped up and whipped around in the direction of the far edge of the meadow where it joined the trees.

"They're here," she said, a smile adding depth to her wrinkles.

My eyes followed hers. Just barely poking out of the grass were two fuzzy heads. To my surprise, as I watched them, they began to edge in closer. Usually rabbits shy away from people. After seeing the way the two of them were staring at us so quizzically, I found myself smiling, too.

When they were about ten feet away from us they stopped abruptly and sat motionless, staring directly at the old woman. She stared back at them, shifting her gaze back and forth from one to the other.

In response, the two rabbits tilted their heads from side to side as though deep in thought. Then, just as suddenly, they turned their backs on us and scampered back into the forest.

"Oh great, we missed them!" I wailed. This catching rabbits wasn't a bit fun.

The old woman simply snatched her two cages and yelled over her shoulder, "Try to keep up if you can."

I laughed to myself. This old woman thinks she can catch up with a pair of rabbits? They could be anywhere by now. And then, she was challenging me, a healthy young kid, to keep up?

By the time I picked up my cages, she was almost out of sight. She had jogged across the meadow like a marathon runner. I had never seen anything like it.

As she wove effortlessly through the dense forest following the pair of rabbits, I about burst a lung trying to keep pace. Not only that, but, I'm embarrassed to say, I kept tripping over rocks and tree roots. She glided in and out of the trees as though she'd been born there.

Before long, I could barely catch sight of her and began to fear I'd be left alone, stranded . . . lost in the forest forever.

CHAPTER SIX

Catching Rabbits

At last she stopped near the base of a large tree. By the time I finally reached her, the old woman was already kneeling by a hole in the ground and had one of the cages open. One of the rabbits was no where in sight and the other appeared to be waiting patiently at the side of the tree.

Then, to my delight and astonishment, out of the hole, one by one, hopped a small army of baby rabbits. Every now and then, the mother rabbit we'd followed would nudge another out with her nose. As each emerged, the old woman gently lifted it and set it carefully in the wire cage. It was the craziest thing! The mother rabbit seemed to be entrusting her babies to the old woman's care. Witnessing this was more than worth the hours I'd spent waiting.

"Like to hold one?" she offered, holding out a fuzzy, grayish-brown body.

Now, no child I knew would ever pass up an opportunity like that. I stretched out my arms eagerly, my fingers trembling with excitement. When she placed the tiny ball of fur in my hands, its fuzzy face tickled my skin and I couldn't help but laugh.

The baby bunnies didn't seem afraid, but they did appear rather dazed and confused. They clearly didn't understand what was going on. After all, nothing like this had happened to them before. The tiny one in my hands raised up on its haunches and looked at me curiously, its nose twitching back and forth as if asking me what was happening. Little did he know, I had no idea what was happening either.

When all the babies were safely in the cage, the old woman gently stroked the head of the mother rabbit. In response, the mother affectionately sniffed the old woman's outstretched hand, then turned and—a little sadly, I thought—crawled back into her hole.

We followed the second rabbit, who had waited patiently the whole time, and the same thing happened. She led us to a second hole, nudged her babies out, and we collected them as before.

By the time we'd finished gathering all the babies, I felt a large, aching knot in my throat. I turned my head away so the old woman couldn't see my sadness.

"Why, whatever is the matter?" she said, her voice still scratchy, but now soft. It seemed I couldn't hide anything from her.

"Why don't the mother rabbits love their babies anymore?" I blubbered, feeling irritated at the way my voice cracked when I spoke.

"Oh, that," she answered. "They do. Believe me, they do. In fact, they love them more than any other rabbits ever have."

I was ashamed at the water building up in my eyes. "Then why are they giving them up?"

The old woman stared at me for a moment. I knew by now that this meant she was thinking hard. "Let's see, how can I put it." She scratched her chin. "Imagine for a moment that you were the parent of a little child. You'd want to do what was best for that child, wouldn't you?"

She waited until I nodded, then continued, "Suppose in order to do what was best for the child it would mean giving him up. Could you do it? Would you do it?"

I thought for a second. "I guess so," I sniffed. "But it would be very sad."

Now she nodded, and I knew she was telling me that was the way the mother rabbits felt, too. "You see," she said, her scratchy voice low and tender, "sometimes you have to do what's best for someone else, even though it hurts."

But I was still confused. "How will they be happier with you, though? Is life in a cage better than living free?"

She bobbed her head sadly up and down. "Sometimes, I'm afraid it is."

"Then, let's take the mother rabbits with us," I said hopefully. "We can put them in the cages, too."

The old woman's eyes grew extra watery as she said, "We can't do it is all, and they know it. It wouldn't work. This is their forest, the place they've always lived. This is where they belong. The babies, on the other hand, are new and fresh. They're better able to adapt to new situations."

"Like life in a cage?"

She nodded. "That too."

I thought for a moment and asked, "You're sure it will be better for the babies this way?"

Without a second of hesitation she answered, "Positive."

I wasn't sure I felt any better about it. After all, I hardly knew the old woman and I didn't fully trust her. Looking back, sometimes I wonder why I ever trusted her at all, especially since she was so strange. At the time, however, I was so caught up with the baby rabbits that I went right back to playing with them, poking the ends of my fingers through the wire cages to stroke their soft fur and noses.

We caged two other batches of bunnies that day, and each time it happened about the same way. The mothers led us to them and turned them over to our keeping. It was weird to have the rabbits come right up to us. What would my friends think if they could see me now, surrounded by baby rabbits, holding them in my own two hands!

When we were finished for the day, I followed the old woman home, toting two of the cages just as before. I was wondering where she would keep them all, especially when her house was already filled up with potted plants.

When we reached the house she again fumbled with the door, opened it, and I followed her inside. As I stepped through the door, I jerked back in surprise. Except for the few pieces of furniture, the house was completely empty; there wasn't a pot, wildflower, pine tree, or weed in sight!

"Where are all the plants?" I asked in amazement, setting the cage of bunnies on the floor.

"Oh, those," she said casually. "They've been replanted."

"All of them?"

"All of them."

I couldn't believe it. I edged over to the window and peered out into the yard. I couldn't see anything planted out front. I gazed out a back window; nothing there either.

I tried again. "They've all been replanted? All the ones that were here yesterday? Every single one of them?"

"Yep," she said, fiddling with the cages. Then, looking up and seeing me stare out the window, she added, "You won't find them out there, if that's what you're looking for."

I waited for an explanation. As usual, she gave me none.

When I turned back around to see what she was doing, I was immediately struck with an odd feeling. Out in the meadow I'd been so preoccupied with the bunnies that I hadn't really paid much attention to her. Now, I noticed there was something strange about her: she looked *too much* the same. For one thing, she was wearing the exact outfit she'd worn all the other days, but that wasn't the weird part. Her hair was precisely the same, *too much* the same. Pieces had fallen out of the bun and hung down over her eyes and the sides of her face in *exactly* the same way. And then, looking down at her feet, the panty hose were sagging around her ankles in *precisely* the same manner—as though each wrinkle was sealed in place. And the knot at the back of her apron was tied in the same loose, sloppy fashion with the ends *just* the lengths they'd been on the other days. An eerie, almost supernatural chill raced up my spine.

Then, I relaxed as it occurred to me that perhaps she slept in her clothes and just got up in the morning without having to change. I had to admit it was a good idea. It would definitely save time. I'd even tried it myself, but Mom didn't seem to appreciate the time saving-value in it. Or maybe it was just my imagination. After all, I'd been around her so much lately that the days were starting to blur together. Still, when I glanced at her and saw the "sameness," I couldn't help shuddering.

When I looked around at the caged bunnies and thought of the missing plants, the weird feeling in me increased. Suddenly, I felt afraid of the old woman. I hardly even knew her. I had to get out of there.

Pretending to check my watch, I stammered, "I—I promised my mom I'd be home early for dinner tonight, so I've got to leave now." It was a lie; I admit it, but it was the only excuse I could come up with.

She eyed me suspiciously, and I felt my face flush from the embarrassment of being caught, but she merely nodded and said, "Very well, then."

On the way home I worked myself into a panic. Was she stealing wild plants and animals and selling them for money? Was I now an accomplice to her crime? I could feel my heart racing. I remembered the sad faces of the mother rabbits and felt partly responsible for their sorrow. And why must the babies be taken from their mothers? For what cause or purpose? Something odd was happening, something I couldn't understand.

Arriving home, I tried to shove the whole thing into the back of my mind. After dinner, I slipped out to the back lawn to visit the stars. JayAnn and Mick had gone to visit their cousins. Sassy was inside because Mom was giving her a bath. Sassy hates baths—she thinks they're a waste of time. Her muffled screams echoed out through the screen door.

So it was just me.

I squinted at the stars and wondered if there was another person out there on another planet looking back at me. I wished there was, and I wished I could ask that person whether I should trust the old lady or not.

The stars had a soothing effect on me. I decided I was overreacting. After all, I really didn't know what the old lady had done with the plants. But from now on I would keep a close eye on her, that's for sure.

Then I remembered the long wait in the meadow and the fun of seeing the bunnies. And to think I had complained and almost gone home! There are some things that are definitely worth waiting for.

Those were the last thoughts that drifted through my head as I stumbled up the steps of our back porch to go to bed.

CHAPTER SEVEN

Owner of the House

When I reached the field the next day I expected to find her working or sitting on the large rock, waiting for me as usual. Much to my disappointment, the field was empty. Hiding my bike in the bushes, I meandered through the field and even beyond the meadow in search of her. She was nowhere to be found. I turned and headed over towards her house, thinking perhaps she'd taken the day off or was sick at home. If nothing else, I wanted to play with the bunnies again. Then I happened to glance up at the big hill.

Pausing to remember our hike to the top a day or two ago, I thought about the big homes where all the important people lived. My parents had driven me through the area countless times to admire the fancy houses, gardens, and tennis courts. It was what they dreamed of owning some day. Then I thought about the poor area. I'd never even seen most of it. Nobody wanted to go there. Mom and Dad said it was dangerous, though I don't know why.

An image of the shabby, junky house I'd seen from the top of the hill flashed into my mind, and for a second I could picture it so clearly it was as if I was still looking down on it. I remembered how it was all alone—set off by itself as though no other house wanted to venture too near for fear its condition might be contagious. It was so run-down, it seemed likely nobody lived there. Maybe it was deserted. Suddenly I had an overwhelming urge to find out.

I thought I could remember about where it was located, though I had never had any reason to go there before. All of the good stores, restaurants, and theaters were on the other side of town. It was an area parents tried to keep their children away from. Picturing it as a great adventure, I found myself excited to explore the area, even mysteriously drawn to it.

The house was harder to find than I'd originally expected. Though I hate to admit it, I finally located it by judging the houses along the way. If they began to improve in appearance, I knew I was headed in the wrong direction. If boarded up windows and peeling, unpainted porches began to appear, I knew I was on the right track.

Pedaling through the neighborhoods, I started to feel more and more uncomfortable. All the little kids seemed to be staring at me. I was a misfit, someone who stood out from the crowd instead of just your ordinary kid. Obviously, something about me seemed out of place or I'm sure I wouldn't have attracted so much attention.

I told myself it was all my imagination. Maybe, I just thought they were staring at me because *I* felt out of place. Ignoring their gazes, I kept my eyes straight ahead and tried to act natural. But it was no use. I could still feel their piercing stares.

As long as I'd come so far, there was no way I was turning back. The deeper I pedaled into the unknown area, the more uneasy I became, and yet my feelings didn't make sense since no one ever threatened me in the least.

Before long, I thought I figured out why the kids were looking at me. It wasn't me they were staring at— it was my bike. They were gazing at it with big, hungry eyes. It was then that I realized I hadn't seen another child on a bike for many blocks. Thinking back, there was only one kid riding an old, beat-up, rusty-looking thing—nothing at all like my bright new one.

Though I knew I was only an average sort of kid, I started to feel like a snob. I felt guilty that I had something they didn't. How I wished I had walked instead of taken my bike. Too late for that, though; I'd have to make the best of it. Besides, it was too far away to go on foot.

At last I came to a long stretch of dumpy-looking property where there were no houses at all, only fields littered with junk, grass clippings, and weeds. At the far end of the dirt road was the place I'd been looking for. Even from a distance I could tell it was the right one; not many homes have toilets sitting on their front lawns.

As I got nearer, I could tell the house was even worse than I'd imagined. Up close, details showed up that were easy to miss from way up on the hill. Old tires were strewn here and there over the property. Some of them were torn apart. Many of the windows had cracked glass or were missing panes. The roof sagged in the middle and a whole section of it was missing. Pieces of old car parts slumped into the dirt by the side of the road in front. Worst of all, the house itself was a hideous mixture of colors, as if any old paint or piece of material handy had been used to make random repairs.

I was now absolutely certain nobody lived there; it was too awful. Nothing, except maybe rats, rodents, and cockroaches, could live in a place so disgusting. It did, however, look like an interesting place to explore. So I inched up slowly.

I was wrong. Someone did live there. I could hear angry voices shouting back and forth from inside the house. It startled me, and I quickly pulled my bike behind some shrubs at the side of the yard. Stepping down from the bike, I peeked out through a hole in the branches.

Looking back, I don't know why I didn't turn around right then and race for home. Something seemed to keep me there. Maybe it was simply curiosity. Maybe it was fate. Or perhaps I just wanted to see what sort of person could live there.

It didn't take long to find out. Barely hanging on its hinges, the screen door burst open violently and slammed against the front of the house. A fat, sloppy-looking man holding a can in his hand staggered out through the doorway and plopped down on a weather-beaten couch which rested awkwardly on what was left of the porch.

Just as suddenly, the man stood back up, yelled some curses at the couch, and kicked it a few times before settling himself at the other end. I could see a spot where a spring had poked up through the cushions. Stuffing was hanging out of its many small and large holes.

The can he carried in his hand hissed as he popped it open. He took a few gulps and burped loudly. Then he settled down into what appeared to be a deep sleep, his fat belly rising and falling as it hung out beneath his short, tank top undershirt. I was glad he was asleep; I was sure if he saw me spying on him he'd murder me.

The other voice I'd heard had sounded like a woman's, but I never saw her at all. I wondered why she would choose to stay inside the house when its interior was most likely at least as bad as the outside.

I don't know what possessed me, but I just had to check out the back of the house. I crept carefully, quietly towards the side of the yard, keeping one eye on the sleeping man on the porch until he was out of sight.

Around back, a small stream ran down one edge of the property. (At least there was one good thing about the place.) I wondered if it was the same stream that passed through the meadow. At the edge of the water, I could see that someone was crouched among the bushes and trees. Perhaps it was the woman from the house. Maybe she had slipped out the back way to get some fresh air.

All at once, the person started to talk, and I realized I was hearing, not a woman's voice, but a boy's. A moment later, the soft, fuzzy outlines of a pair of rabbits came into view. The boy was talking to them and appeared to be feeding them part of his lunch. From so far away, his voice was muffled and I couldn't hear what he was saying. It looked like he had a carrot stick in his hand. He held it out to them and they were letting him stroke their tiny heads. It reminded me of the old woman. Up until now, she was the only one I'd ever seen do that with wild animals.

The boy shifted positions. As he reached back for another piece of carrot, I could see his head and face for the first time.

Instantly, my body went numb. I was so startled by what I saw I could hardly breathe. It was a face I recognized, one I had seen many times before. It was Bud!

My first impulse was to dash over and warn him about the mean guy sitting on the front porch. But before I could move, pictures and thoughts started to connect themselves in my mind. I saw Bud the week before, a faded bruise on his head. I saw him limping as he came to play games on Mick and JayAnn's front lawn. I saw him safeguarding his treasure in a dented soup can. Instantly, it all made sense. Though it seemed too horrible to be true, I knew it was.

I felt sick to my stomach. Bud was too nice a person to live in a gross place like this. It wasn't fair. Bud always seemed so cheerful and happy. Nobody could grin like he could; it was one of his best features. He couldn't possibly live here. But he did. I now knew that he did.

The words of the old woman echoed in my memory: "I tell you, that Bud is a Jewel of the Nile . . ."

Now I knew what she meant. Bud was surrounded by all this dirt and garbage, yet he didn't fit in. A sloppy, violent looking man dozed on the front porch, and here, just around the corner, Bud was gently feeding his lunch to his rabbit friends.

I kept telling myself I should leave. I kept telling myself it was none of my business. Most of all, I was certain Bud would be horrified if he knew I'd seen him like this. He'd probably stop coming around. He'd be too embarrassed to ever show up again. I would if it had been me.

Still, I remained, frozen to the spot, completely mesmerized by the sight . . . feeling sorry for Bud.

CHAPTER EIGHT

Dog Money

I'm not sure how long I remained there, gaping like an idiot, watching Bud. Before long, he finished feeding the rabbits and moved over by the stream. To my horror, he got down on his stomach and dipped his entire head into what must have been icy cold water, then scrubbed and scrubbed his hair and face. At least it was summer and the hot sun would dry and warm him soon. I wondered what he did in the winter.

I felt sick and ashamed. For several years I had known Bud, been friends with him, played tag with him. We had explored the Nile together countless times. And yet, all this time I'd known absolutely nothing about him. Bud had simply been "good old Bud," nothing else. Now that I knew one of his deepest secrets he seemed like so much more.

Suddenly I couldn't get out of there fast enough. I crept back to where I'd stashed my bike and pedaled away so fast I thought the muscles in my legs would snap. I zoomed past the staring faces of the children, whizzed past the cracked windows and peeling porches. I didn't want to see any of it.

I didn't slow down until I reached the borders of my own neighborhood. Then I took a deep breath of relief.

When I barged through my own front door, Mom said, "Hi, honey. You're just in time for lunch."

I was still trying to catch my breath and couldn't answer her.

"Well, dear," Mom scowled, "you certainly look worn out! What have you been doing?"

I couldn't tell her I had just run away from Bud's house, and Bud's father, and Bud's neighborhood, and all the children with the big hungry eyes, so instead I gasped out, "I just got real hungry."

Mom chuckled. "Well, good. You're just in time then. I haven't seen much of you lately anyway." She gave me a big hug and helped me take off my jacket.

I thought of the poor woman at Bud's place, screaming and sobbing from inside the broken-down house. I returned Mom's big hug and she led me into the kitchen to eat lunch.

As I gulped down my sandwich, the events of the morning kept rolling through my mind. When Mom offered me some carrot sticks, I slipped a few into my pocket.

After lunch I hurried upstairs to where I keep my piggy bank. It's where I store my "dog money." Awhile ago, Mom promised me that if I could save up enough money she'd let me buy a puppy from the pet store. I've been begging her for one all of my life. Up until recently, she'd said I was too young to take care of a dog, but a few months ago she said I was now old enough—and ever since I've been saving my money like mad. I was about half way there and could hardly wait.

Yanking the rubber plug from the bottom of the pig, I dumped the coins and scattered the dollar bills out on my bedspread. I fingered it sadly as I counted it, then stuffed most of it into my pocket—the one without the carrot sticks. I sighed. Maybe someday I'd be able to save up the money again.

Soon I was back on my bike heading for a small gift shop not far from our neighborhood. When I got there, I walked up and down every aisle until I found exactly what I was looking for. There on a shelf in the back corner sat some medium-sized wooden storage boxes. I picked one up. The lid was attached to the bottom of the box with shiny gold hinges, and a matching latch held the front closed. It even came with a lock and a small gold key with a hole through the top so it could be worn on a chain around one's neck. It was far better than my treasure box. It was even better than Mick's fishy tackle box. It was the best treasure box I could imagine.

I lugged the box over to the candy section, where I selected a sucker shaped like a ring with an enormous jewel on it, an elastic watch with a candy face, and a small bag of chocolate, gold foil-wrapped coins.

After purchasing the items, I took them home. When I opened the box the key turned perfectly in the lock. I placed the candy inside and re-locked it, leaving the key sticking out. Then, with a black marker, across the front edge of the box in small letters I wrote: BUD.

Meanwhile, Sassy, dying to know what was in the sack, kept pounding on my door trying to get in. I had to lean hard against it and brace a chair under the knob so she couldn't push it open.

I bundled the box up in my jacket so Sassy couldn't see it, dragged the chair away from the door, and squeezed quickly past her. She clamped her hands tightly onto my pants, but I managed to break free.

"What you got there? What're you doing in there?" Sassy yelled after me. "What's in your jacket? I wanna see!"

She trailed me outside. I hopped on my bike.

"I wanna come, too," she pleaded. "Please . . . please!"

I have to admit, I felt guilty doing it, but I turned and said, "None of your business, Sassy." Then I sped off.

I knew I couldn't take her with me, for sure not this time. Mom would kill me if she knew where I was going, let alone if I took Sassy along. And I was sure the little pest would tell; she blabs everything. And I didn't want her to know about Bud, either. That was a secret I'd take to my grave if I could. I was certain I'd never tell Mick and JayAnn. Mick would probably be okay with it, but JayAnn wouldn't have a thing to do with Bud if she knew.

As I rode off, Sassy bawled and ran after me for a few yards, still begging to come. I started to feel even worse. What did she do all day, anyway? (Besides get into trouble, I mean.) In her age group, there weren't any kids nearby for her to play with. Besides, she only liked to play with us big kids—though the feeling, unfortunately, was not mutual. Yes, she was obnoxious; yes, she was annoying; but she looked so sad and frustrated as she stumbled along clumsily behind me, her face all red and tear-stained. I promised myself to make an extra effort to play with her for a while when I got home.

When I reached Bud's house for the second time that day, I marched directly around back. I didn't want to look at the house again or hear the people fighting. Luckily, the yard was empty now. Creeping over to the spot where I'd seen him playing with the rabbits, I set the box just inside the bushes where I was sure he would find it. Then I took the carrots from my pocket and set them next to the box.

I don't remember much about the ride home. It was more like floating. I do, however, remember passing by the field once more to check for any sign of the old woman. There was still no one there. I wondered what had happened to her. I feared that I might not see her again.

At home, I remembered my promise about playing with Sassy. Usually she practically attacks me when I walk through the door. This time, however, I couldn't find her anywhere.

Mom informed me that Sassy wasn't feeling well and had gone to bed. I found that hard to believe. Sassy never gets sick; she's too ornery to be sick. Even germs don't like to be around her. She must be faking, I thought to myself.

"By the way, your comic books came today," Mom said. "I put them on your bed."

I raced to my room and flopped down on my bed. They were there all right, but someone else had found them first. In dark magic marker, someone had drawn mustaches, earrings, and sharp teeth all over the faces of the Happy Heroes on the covers. Sassy!

For a moment I was absolutely furious. Then I remembered her pathetic face, all flushed and dejected as she ran along behind my bike. Someone was either faking being sick, or else someone was very unhappy.

I made my way down the hall and slid one of the comic books under Sassy's door, making sure it stuck part way out where I could see it. I watched until I saw it disappear.

I longed to sit and read one of the other comics, but it was getting late and I was too tired to think. Besides, with all that had happened, I didn't think I could really enjoy them today. I tucked the comic books under my jacket, figuring I'd take them with me to the field the next day in case we had a long wait in the meadow again.

Later that night, while brushing my teeth, I wondered where the old woman had been. I hoped she'd be back tomorrow.

Just before climbing into bed, I went to the window and made a wish upon the stars. I wished that someday I'd have enough money for a puppy.

CHAPTER NINE

The Trouble With Heroes

Mick and JayAnn had been asking about me—wondering where I'd been lately and all. It must have seemed odd to them, my being gone so much. Usually we spend most of our free time together.

Actually, to tell the truth, I was purposefully avoiding them. For some reason I didn't want them to find out about the strange old lady. I guess everyone likes to have some secrets they keep to themselves. Or maybe it was just that I didn't want to have to share her with anyone else.

It's surprising, when I think back, that Mom didn't ask more questions about where I was going. Maybe she would have if she hadn't been so distracted with other "Mom things." And Sassy always seemed to wear her out. Besides, during the school year I'd often meet new friends who lived further away. A lot of times I'd stay at their houses for lunch or dinner and play with them the whole day. I imagine it didn't seem all that unusual to her. Anyway, as long as I remained safe and sound, what was there to worry about? Our part of town was relatively safe during the day—and she didn't know about my frequent excursions into the other neighborhoods.

An early, bright summer morning greeted me as I stretched and flung myself out of bed. I feel guilty admitting this after the promise I'd made, but I wanted to strike out extra early in order to avoid another run-in with Sassy. Scarfing down a quick bowl of cereal, I grabbed my jacket and the comic books and headed to the garage for my bike. I had left a message on the counter so Mom wouldn't think I'd been kidnapped.

I'd just begun to pedal up the street when I suddenly got the feeling I was being followed. Turning my head ever so slightly and glancing out of the corner of my eye, I could see Mick and JayAnn, both on bikes, pedaling silently about a hundred yards behind. Every so often, they'd pull up next to bushes and houses, trying hard not to be seen. It reminded me of the time we'd spied on the kids up the street because they kept throwing rotten apples at us.

Pretending not to notice, I pedaled along, never changing my pace; only, instead of heading straight to the field as planned, I turned left after just a few blocks so they would think I was going towards town.

Figuring it would take them awhile to catch up since they were keeping a safe distance, I pulled quietly through Mr. Jameston's backyard and circled around to where I could see them through the hedges. They passed by, then turned left, just as I had. Bewildered that I was no where in sight, they pulled off the road to discuss the matter.

I could hear them talking. It made me want to laugh so badly that I had to bite my tongue so the pain would distract me. It's so much harder to keep from laughing when you know you can't, like at church or in the library or when you're hiding from someone.

"Guess we might as well go home," Mick said.

Although she is a year younger than Mick, JayAnn, always has to be in charge of everything. She replied sharply, "No way. Keep going. We'll search every street we pass."

I could tell by the look on Mick's face that he'd rather give up and go home, but, as usual, he followed reluctantly behind, obeying JayAnn's strict commands.

By that time, I was clamping my mouth shut with both hands and biting my tongue so hard I thought it might bleed. I was anxious to get out of there before I blew my cover.

After they turned down one of the side streets to look for me, I squeezed my bike through the hedges and sped off towards the field. I wondered if the old lady would be back today. I knew I'd be disappointed if she wasn't.

When I pulled into the field, I was relieved to see her sitting on the same rock with some more wire cages. I was especially glad to see the cages, since I'd had even more fun collecting the rabbits than I'd had digging up the plants. Once again, the idea hit me that she looked exactly the same every time I saw her. I mean, *more* than just the same. A lot of people look mostly the same every day, but there was something too perfect about her imperfect appearance that was difficult to figure out.

I couldn't help smiling when I saw her—I was so relieved. Somehow, the days spent with the old lady were becoming important to me. For one thing, it was fun to have an adult's undivided attention. And I think she liked me too, for I saw the corner of her mouth rise ever so slightly when she saw me.

"Did you have somewhere else you had to go yesterday?" (I couldn't help asking. I've always been a curious person.)

Her answer surprised me. "No," she said. "You did." Those three words and the sly look on her face seemed to imply so much more.

I knew instantly, right then and there, that she knew exactly where I'd been the day before. I was also certain, without a doubt, that she knew full well about my secret gift to Bud. But how? That I did not know.

My mind raced backward, reliving my travels of the day before. No, there was no way she could have followed me—I was pretty sure of that. But somehow she knew. I was positive that she knew. The only thing I could think of was that perhaps she'd been working in the trees somewhere behind Bud's house and had seen me there. Of course, yes, that must be it. She'd spied on me through the bushes, just as I'd spied on Bud.

"Did you find what you were looking for?" she asked, searching my face as she spoke.

I wanted her to know that I was on to her game, so I simply said, "I have a feeling you already know that I did."

Though normally she manages to hide her feelings, this time she seemed just a little shocked at my answer, as though it bothered her that I might know something I shouldn't. Then her mouth widened into the biggest wrinkly grin I'd ever seen. I noticed a brief flash in her eyes, as if she admired my spunk and couldn't help being amused by my words. Then, without another word, she stood up, lifted two of the cages, and headed in the direction of the meadow. She knew I'd pick up the other two and follow behind.

When we arrived, the meadow practically sparkled. It seemed different, even more striking than before. Part of me knew that was impossible, since only a day had passed. At the same time, in other ways, I felt like I was visiting an old, familiar friend.

Like last time, we wandered around the meadow for a while, cooled our feet in the stream, then settled down for what I suspected would be another long wait. The woman pulled out some large purple grapes and some juicy strawberries for us to snack on. It was then that I remembered my comic books, which I'd rolled up and stuffed into the front of my jacket. I had just stretched out on my stomach and was smoothing one of them open to the first page when she looked over my shoulder. In her now familiar scratchy voice, she asked, "What's that you've got there?"

"Comic books," I answered proudly. Then, thinking myself rude, I added, "Would you like to look at one?" I held one of the others out to her and she accepted it between two bony fingers.

"What're they about?" she asked, giving the cover a sidelong glance.

"They're about heroes, mostly. You know, people with special powers and stuff."

"Mmph," she mumbled, settling down next to me and spreading open the cover.

For half an hour or so we read in complete silence. Occasionally, the old woman stopped to rub her eyes and close them tightly as though they hurt. I was just getting mesmerized by the story, forgetting where I actually was, when the sound of her harsh voice startled me, interrupting my thoughts.

"Trash," she said sharply, tossing the book on to the ground by my face.

I sat up in surprise. "What?!"

"You heard me," she said. "Trash. Those books are complete and utter trash."

Well, now I was really offended. After all, those were my heroes she was talking about. I dreamed of being like them. And it wasn't just me; all my friends loved them, too.

"It's not trash," I stated defensively, my voice loud and almost hostile. I reached down and snatched it up protectively. "They're great stories. Everyone thinks so. Who asked you, anyway?"

I shouldn't have said anything so rude to an adult, but the old lady didn't seem nearly so lofty nor as touchy as other grownups. She wasn't the type to be upset by a difference of opinion.

"Trash," she said again, shaking her head in that way I'd seen old people do thousands of times. It was the head shake that meant, "Kids nowadays, what's the matter with them?" At least that's how it seemed to me.

"Those are my heroes!" I practically shrieked.

"Your heroes?!" she answered back. "What could possibly make those silly, absurd creatures anybody's heroes?"

I was quick to defend myself. (In anger, I always talk way too fast.) "They're great. They have all sorts of special powers. One of them can run super fast, another is really strong, and one can see right through walls. And not only that, they can do all sorts of other neat things, and they're very, very, brave!" With those words, I turned my back on her.

"Brave! Ha!" she said sternly. I could see she wasn't the type to back down in an argument. "Let me ask you this: If you had all sorts of special powers would it be easier or harder for you to be brave?"

I thought for a second. "Easier."

"Then who wouldn't be brave if they had all sorts of extra-special powers?"

The truth hit me like a brick. I saw her point instantly, but still was so cross that I didn't say a word. She just didn't understand.

When I didn't answer, she questioned me again. This time I answered quietly. Looking at the ground, I mumbled, "I guess everyone would."

She tapped the corner of the comic book in my hand and added, "If everyone would, then tell me what's so special about them?"

She didn't give me time to answer, but continued, "Anyone would dare to chase down some bandit if they knew they were faster and stronger than their enemy. Ha! For that matter, who wouldn't be brave enough to barge into a room if they could see through the walls and already knew what was inside? I tell you, it's pure insanity to call such people heroes. Besides, they don't even exist, so how can you ever hope to be like them? If you're sitting around dreaming of being able to shoot darts out of your nose, let me just tell you right now, give it up, honey, 'cause it's not going to happen."

I was fascinated by the old woman's reasoning. Odd as she was, she did make some sense.

"Well," I said at last, "then who are your heroes?"

She tipped her head back in thought for a moment, then asked, "Have you ever been down to McMathew's store?"

"Of course," I answered, feeling a little smug that she seemed to be changing the subject.

"Ever see the man who sells newspapers out front?"

I knew who she was talking about. A man in an electric wheelchair sat in front of the store most afternoons with a stack of newspapers and a moneybox. His head flops over limply to one side. It's almost impossible to understand him when he talks, but I've heard that if you really stop and listen to him long enough you'll begin to understand. People say he tells some real funny jokes and stories. Bud's told a few of them to me. I've always been a little afraid of the man. I guess because he's different. I'm never sure how to act around him.

"You mean Luther?"

She pointed a bony finger at me. "That's the one. Now there's a hero for you!"

Luther, a hero? The idea was ridiculous. Luther could hardly do anything. Who'd ever want to be like him?

I figured I'd force her to prove her answer. "What do you mean?"

She didn't even hesitate. She looked me in the eye and said, "Every morning it takes Luther two or three hours, even with the help of a live-in aide, to get out of bed, eat breakfast, get dressed, and climb into his wheelchair. It takes another hour for him to get out of his apartment, down the elevator, and guide himself up the street to the front of the store. Then he sits there all day, stuck in his hot, sticky wheelchair, while other people rush past—playing, shopping, driving cars, riding bikes. He sits there in bad weather and in good because he wants to have a job and earn his keep."

She paused to make sure I understood what she was saying, then continued, "It's very hard for Luther to talk, but he tries to anyway, even though most people don't take the time to understand him. And what does he talk about? Does he complain about his miserable condition? No. He tells funny jokes, poems, and stories to cheer people up. He sits there all day, every day, with people staring at him as they walk by, children pointing at him and giggling, and still he remains cheerful. How many so-called ordinary people do you know who are as brave and kind as that?"

I couldn't think of a single one. "None, I guess." It came out almost in a whisper.

She nodded in agreement. Then she said, "Is it easier for a crippled man or a normal man to walk down the street? Is it easier for a beautiful woman or a homely one to show her face in public? Does it take more courage for a healthy man or a sick one to get up in the morning and face a new day? Those are the kind of questions to ask yourself when you're searching for bravery."

"I think I understand what you mean," I said. "You're saying that people who have problems have to be much braver than those who have special powers."

She smiled a knowing smile. "That's just it. When you look for a hero, don't look for one that has more and does less. Find one that *has less* and *does more*. Those are the real heroes."

I wondered how she knew so much about Luther—and Bud, too, for that matter. I didn't feel like reading my comic books anymore. They seemed lifeless and dull. Besides, it was pretty easy to figure out what would happen—they always end the same way. I thought maybe I'd take them down to Luther some day. Maybe he'd enjoy reading them as he sat and waited.

Or maybe I'd just give them to Sassy and let her draw all over them.

CHAPTER TEN

A Day of Squirrels

About an hour or so later, as we were eating lunch, a couple of squirrels scampered out from the trees. I thought I'd try to offer them a taste of my lunch as I'd seen Bud do with the rabbits, but the old woman had other plans.

"They're waiting for us," she announced, picking up her cages.

I naturally assumed this meant we were collecting squirrels today instead of rabbits. Knowing by now I'd have to be quick or risk getting left behind, I dropped my sandwich, grabbed the other cages, and took off after her.

The rest of the day was a lot like the former one, except this time it was squirrels instead of bunnies. Once again, the adults willingly gave up their babies. I never got used to it. I always felt so bad for the mothers as I watched them slink mournfully away through the bushes, alone and childless. I still couldn't figure out why it had to happen.

But it was sure fun! There is nothing like holding a baby animal, be it rabbit or squirrel, in the palm of your hand. And I was learning so much. I wished school would be more like this instead of merely seeing pictures of animals or reading about them in textbooks.

By late afternoon, the cages were overflowing with baby squirrels. I wondered how they'd get along with the old lady's pet rabbits. I hoped she'd transfer them to bigger cages so they wouldn't be so crowded. Again I wondered why the old woman needed quite so many pets. These thoughts floated through my brain as I helped her lug the cages back to her house.

When we got inside, I immediately looked around for the cages with the rabbits. "Where'd you put them?" I asked, my eyes darting desperately from one side of the room to the other.

"Put what?"

"The baby bunnies."

"Oh, them. They're gone."

My heart sank; my stomach lurched. I felt like I'd been punched really hard. A sensation of panic flooded through my body like a jolt of electricity. Disappearing plants are one thing; animals are quite another. What was going on? My concern for the animals was intense.

"Where'd you take them?" I choked out.

She didn't answer my question. Instead, she pointed toward the corner where the rabbits had been and casually said, "You can set those cages right over there."

A wild urge to run out of the front door, open the cages, and set the squirrels free surged through me. Fear, distrust, and anger churned within me. Still, I'm ashamed to say, I did nothing—just stood there staring at the floor. Then, after a minute or two, I set the cages down.

An idea had entered my head, a way to find out for myself exactly what was happening to the plants and animals. As best as I could, I masked my feelings and tried to act natural.

I backed away towards the door and—again—lied. "My mom's been mad at me because I'm always gone so much. I'd better leave."

Moms are great for blaming things on when you're in a pinch. In truth, however, it was getting late. All I knew was I had to get away from there. I'd be able to think much better at home. Anyway, the longer I stayed the greater the chance that the old woman would begin to sense my true feelings.

"All right," was all she said, giving me one of her slightly amused looks.

On the way home I thought about my plan and how I would carry it out. By the time I walked through the front door I pretty much had the whole thing figured out. But it would have to wait until later—much later—long after dark.

During dinner with my family, I reluctantly remembered the promise I'd made to myself about Sassy. She was sitting across the table from me, opening her mouth on purpose so I could see all the gross, chewed up food inside. Yuck! If only she wasn't so annoying . . . but a promise was a promise, even if it was to myself. I might as well get it over with.

"Hey, Sassy," I said, attempting to sound cheerful. "Let's go over and get Mick and JayAnn and play tag."

She shot me an odd-looking stare, full of suspicion and disbelief. "All right," she finally said, still looking slightly distrustful. Then her face beamed a little. She looked a lot less irritating that way.

We played all sorts of games out on the lawn that night: Tag, Red Rover, Statue Maker, Cops and Robbers, Martians and Witches. Although I fully expected him to come, Bud never showed up that night. With a shudder, I pictured him in that beat-up house with the crying woman inside and the angry man plopped on the couch out front. I felt the urge to go and find him, but I knew there was no telling where Bud might be. I had a feeling he didn't spend much time at home.

I thought back to the first time I saw him, how he'd wandered by one afternoon while we were exploring the Nile. He just kind of joined in, not in any pushy sort of way, almost as though he'd always been one of us. After that, he continued to come back. I was glad.

He provided a nice balance to JayAnn's bossy, pushy, "always have to have everything her own way" personality. Mick, he's so used to JayAnn ordering him around that he doesn't seem to know how to think for himself. Bud, however, is his own person, kind of independent, does his own thing. At the same time, he's always pleasant and never fights with anyone. He's peaceful to be around. I wondered if he'd end up a lot like Mr. Edgar some day.

When Mom called us in for the night, I pulled on my pajamas, climbed into bed, and waited until I heard her crack my door open to check on me. When she came, I pretended to be sound asleep. Then I stayed awake for a couple of hours until I saw the light go off in my parents' room down the hall.

I waited a little bit longer, just to be sure. It was hard to stay awake. It had been a tiring day. My eyelids kept drooping closed.

Eventually I climbed out of bed and slipped back into my clothes. Retrieving my flashlight from under my bed, I felt my way down the dark hallway to the closet by the door and took out my thickest, warmest coat. It was summer and still pretty warm at night, but if I had to stay outside very long, I might end up needing it. Plus, it would double as a soft place to sit.

I took a deep breath and hoped I was doing the right thing. Sometimes it was easy to know what was right;

other times the answer wasn't nearly so clear. All I knew was that I needed to find out exactly what was going on.

As quietly as I could, I slipped out the door into the cool night air.

CHAPTER ELEVEN

Light in the Window

The empty street, dark and shadowy, took on a sinister, supernatural quality in the night. As I crept up the sidewalk towards the old woman's house, I wished more than ever that I had a dog. He would be a companion and protector at times like these.

The trees, which were quite ordinary in the daylight, seemed to be moving and twisting in the blackness. I could easily imagine claw-like branches and gnarled fingers reaching out to grab me. The houses, looking lonely and deserted, were nearly all dark. I began to feel I was somewhere else, somewhere far away where I'd never been before, instead of walking up the same street I've seen every day of my life. It was a lonely feeling. No one seemed to exist but me.

By the time I got to the field, I was terrified. (It's one of the curses of having too good of an imagination.)

I paused at the edge and peered across to my dark destination. It seemed at least five times as far away as in the daytime. Who knows what could be lurking out in the shadows among the trees and bushes? My feet were frozen to the ground, as though I'd lost the power to control them. Each time I commanded them to step into the field, they refused. And then, even worse, I started to remember all the horrible stories I'd heard on the news about bad things happening to people who just happened to be out alone at night.

I'm sure I would have turned around right then and raced for home if I hadn't suddenly pictured the fuzzy, innocent faces of the bunnies and squirrels who would, all because of my lack of courage, end up who knows where. I forced myself to start walking across the pitch-black earth. Now I was really wishing for a dog by my side.

I imagine there was probably another way to get to the old woman's house besides crossing through the field, but in the dark I didn't want to risk getting lost in a strange neighborhood. Besides, (I kept telling myself) any minute I'd make it to the other side, if I just kept going.

The blackness was so thick that within seconds I felt like I was losing my sense of direction. Hadn't I just passed that tree? Was I walking in circles? I felt a floating, unreal sensation, as though I was caught up in a dream.

The trees at the opposite end of the field created a strange illusion against the nearly lightless sky, as if the longer I walked the further away they became. It was like passing through one of those endless tunnels they have in horror movies—the ones where the guy keeps running and running but can't reach the light at the end.

At last I reached the spot where the trees bordered the old woman's house. Gathering all my courage, I sucked in a deep breath and plowed through the middle of them as fast as I could.

It was a mistake. Running made me feel even worse, like something was chasing me—even though I was pretty sure nothing was there. It was the same way I feel at home when I dart up the stairs from the basement. I'm always sure something is about to reach out and grab my legs or pounce on me from behind.

Once I broke through the trees, I felt a little better. The old woman's house stood off by itself. Somewhere in the house a light was on; a thin strip of faint yellow light fought its way through the horizontal crack between the blind and the base of the window frame. Sneaking up carefully, I peeked through the crack, hoping I wasn't already too late.

A sigh of relief escaped my lips. There they were, the cages, still filled with baby squirrels. The woman was lying face down on the floor next to them, talking to them, and stroking them through the bars with one of her crooked fingers. I wished that I knew what she was saying. Quietly, I backed away from the window and found a spot where I could lean against a tree and still be able to see both the front and back doors of the house.

I knew what I was doing was dangerous. It was risky to be out alone after dark, even for a grownup. I knew I was a fool to take such a chance. If Mom knew about it, she'd be furious. She'd probably lock me in my room at night. And she'd probably be right to do so. I'd seen the news. I'd heard people talk. Kids understand more than grownups think we do. Horrible things went on every day in the city, and even here in the suburbs—especially at night. I also knew I had to stay—for the sake of the animals, if nothing else. I had assisted in their capture. I was partly responsible if something bad happened to them. It was my duty.

Oh how I wished I had a dog with me. He'd have curled up next to me and made me feel safe and less lonely. And he would have barked if anyone tried to sneak up on us.

For a while, I was very afraid. Every time a twig snapped I was sure it was someone coming through the bushes to kill me. Then I happened to look up at the stars. Immediately I felt better. There they were, just like always. Their sameness was comforting. I felt like the stars—or something out there in the vast universe— would protect me. I made a wish on the biggest one—I wished that I'd make it through the night.

Now and then, I'd glance over at the house and I'd see the same thin light slipping out into the blackness. Didn't the old woman ever sleep?

It seemed like a couple of hours had passed when the old woman turned on some more lights in the house and the thin, dim crack of light grew much brighter, changing from pale yellow to a brilliant white. My fear faded as I looked at the brighter, whiter strip of light, and I thought something about it seemed familiar. By chance, I glanced up at the night sky and realized that it reminded me of starlight. Artists sometimes paint the stars yellow—and the moon too—but they're not. They're white . . . a clean, solid, brilliant sort of white against a field of navy blue-black. My eyes shifted back and forth from the window to the stars, comparing the two colors. All the while, I wondered what the old lady was doing in there so late at night with all the lights on when she should be snug in bed.

About half an hour later, the old woman turned off the extra lights and the crack of light once more grew pale and yellow. My eyes blurred; they needed sleep. I had to struggle hard to keep them open.

At least another half-hour passed. I grew bored and restless. I knew I'd better get up and walk around or I'd drift off to sleep. As I stood up, my legs ached and tingled. I stuck one hand out against the tree for balance and waited for the numb feeling to end.

Now that I was up, I thought I might as well take another quick peek through the window. I was curious to see what the old lady was doing.

Craning my neck to peer through the crack, I felt a wave of guilt sweep through me. I knew what I was doing was wrong. People have a right to their privacy. After all, I wouldn't like someone spying on me. Still, this wasn't a normal situation. The old woman wouldn't tell me what was happening to the animals. Under the circumstances, I felt I had a right to know.

Now I could see the old woman perched on the edge of the bed next to the lamp, holding a clipboard with a piece of paper on it, and making marks with a pen. My gaze moved to the kitchen. It was neat and tidy, as always. From there my eyes wandered to the cages with the squirrels.

My heart leapt to my throat. I had to blink two or three times to convince myself it was true. The cages were completely empty. They were sitting exactly as they'd been before, but they were utterly and totally empty! Not a single baby squirrel remained. My eyes darted around the room, scanning the floor, the table, the corners. No squirrels anywhere!

How could it be? I'd been watching the house all night long. They were there in the cages the first time I'd looked; I was sure of it. Nobody had left the house or entered. I would have seen them. Had I drifted off to sleep for a few minutes without realizing it? Where were those squirrels?

By now, I was trembling from fear and exhaustion. Something very weird was going on, and I was caught in the middle of it. My brain ached as I vainly searched for an answer. I couldn't think at all.

I glanced back at the old woman, still sitting by the lamp, working. Her hair was the same. Her clothes were the same. Her stockings were still sagging with the same amount of wrinkles.

I watched as she got up, pulled down the covers of the bed, took off her shoes, and climbed in. Her gnarled hand reached out for the lamp. The room went dark.

Maybe I was having a nightmare. Any minute I'd wake up and find myself leaning against the tree, or even better, home in my own bed. And yet, I'd never felt so awake. My heart was pounding. Thoughts and pictures spun in my head. Suddenly, I wanted to be home, back in my safe, warm bed, more than I'd ever wanted anything.

I can hardly remember going home. I must have run most of the way, because it was as if one moment I was standing in the old woman's yard and the next I was on my front porch turning the knob noiselessly. Bolting the door behind me, I groped my way down the hall to my room.

Lying in bed had never felt so wonderful. I stretched my legs out as far as they would go, all the way to the bottom of the sheets. I turned my face toward the window and thanked the stars for getting me safely home. I tried to take some deep breaths and waited for my heart to stop pounding.

Then, I must have fallen asleep.

CHAPTER TWELVE

The Interview

Dark, lumpy bags were sagging under my eyes when I awoke. The night had passed slowly, broken only by occasional, restless, tormented fits of sleep. Strange nightmares kept drifting through my dreams, visions of the forest animals being captured and used for experiments or fashioned into fur coats. The animals in the nightmares shrieked, groaned, and squealed, their frightened, helpless eyes, begging me to save them. I jerked awake covered with sweat and terrified of the old woman.

I decided I would never go back to the field again.

At breakfast I was cross and depressed. It seemed like I'd been going to the field for months instead of just days. Already I couldn't remember what I used to do before I met the old woman. Instead of eating, I played with my cereal until it got soggy. Sluggishly, I began to read the back of the cereal box. It advertised a contest where you were invited to write an essay about any significant event in history. It was divided into different age groups, and the prize for first place was five hundred dollars. Then it hit me: With a large amount of money like that I could easily buy a dog. If only I could write an outstanding essay. But I didn't know hardly anything about history, except for a few meaningless bits and pieces mentioned in school. I hadn't lived long enough yet.

I hadn't lived long enough . . . I hadn't lived long enough. The words circled through my mind like a whirlpool. It was true—*I* hadn't lived long enough to know much about history—but I knew someone who had. The old woman must be a walking history book. She'd have hundreds of interesting stories to tell. If only I wasn't terrified of her. If only I hadn't decided never to go back.

For the first time in weeks I sat down to watch hour after hour of cartoons. But I couldn't relax. The faces of the animals in my dreams kept haunting me. They needed my help. If I did nothing to save them, I would carry the weight of the blame for the rest of my life. I had to find out what was happening. After all, the old lady hadn't done anything to hurt *me* yet, and she'd had plenty of opportunities to do so. Still, maybe she hadn't hurt me only because she didn't know I was suspicious of her.

I have to admit I was also extremely bored. Sassy kept standing in front of the TV, and I was tired of dragging her away. I was also sick of her putting her feet on me inch by inch when she knows I hate it. She tries to make it look like it's an accident, as though she's merely slipping while stretching, but it's obvious that she does it on purpose.

That helped me make up my mind. I was going. I picked up a pad of paper and a pen on the way out the door. Fortunately, Sassy, who was busy trying to fish something out of the heater vent, hadn't seen me slip out. (I think she was looking for one of Mom's fancy earrings she wasn't supposed to play with.)

When I got to the field, there was the old lady, sitting on the same rock, holding the same, now empty, cages. She must have been waiting for hours.

I was determined to act completely natural, like I suspected nothing. "Been waiting long?" I asked as I stashed my bike in the bushes.

"Nope, just barely got here," she answered. (That was always her answer. She always seemed to know when I was coming.)

"Usually you get here a lot earlier," I added suspiciously, trying to find out as much as I could. But she was one step ahead of me.

"Usually you do, too," she answered, a trace of a mischievous smile creasing her lips in response to how she'd managed to turn things back on me. Then she added, "You look tired. Were you up late?"

Something about the way she spoke the words really bothered me. It was as though she knew a lot more than she was letting on. Or maybe it was my guilty conscience, knowing I'd been spying on her, that caused me to feel that way. Still, this time I wasn't going to let her get the best of me.

"No," I lied, "I feel just great." I wondered why she didn't look even the slightest bit tired. After all, I knew she had also been up all night.

Before long, we were back in the meadow, settling down for the usual wait. Perhaps she really was quite tired, for I saw her close her eyes and squeeze her eyelids tightly again and again. I wondered if her eyes hurt as much as mine did.

Knowing it would probably be a long wait, I decided it was a good time to bring up the contest. "I found an ad for a contest on the back of a cereal box this morning," I began. She turned and looked at me, listening intently as I continued. "I want to write an essay for it and win the prize money so I can buy a dog. I've been saving up for one for the longest time. It's taking forever and I want one real bad."

"Is that so . . . " was all she said.

"Only problem is," I continued, "it has to be about something in history, and I don't know anything about it. But you've been around so long, I thought maybe you'd help me. You know, like maybe I could interview you and ask you some questions."

To my surprise, she chuckled at my request. Then she said, "You can surely ask me anything you'd like, but I doubt I'll be much help."

I figured this was her way of being modest. I know old people love to talk about the past. Once they get started, they can go on and on about the "good old days."

"All right then," I said. "Tell me what it was like during World War II."

"Hmmm," she mumbled, hardly taking any time to think. "Guess I don't know much about that. Except that it was bad, of course."

Was that all she could give me? Talk about stating the obvious. Everybody already knows that the war was "bad." I was stunned. How could someone live through a major war and not know more about it than that? Maybe she used to live in one of the neutral countries. I had to admit, there was something a little unusual about the tone of her voice and the way she talked.

"All right," I tried again. "Then tell me about the first airplanes, what people said about them. That kind of stuff."

"Never been in an airplane," she said. "Never had any reason to."

This was going to be harder than I'd thought. I tried once more. "Okay, how about the Depression?"

"Oh, I don't know much about that," she answered. "I've always been happy."

I looked to see if she was making a joke. If she was trying to be funny, she sure hid it well. Her face remained serious and thoughtful as she shook her head a little and shrugged her shoulders.

"We'll try something a bit more recent, then," I suggested. Perhaps she had that old-person disease that makes them forget things. "What about the sixties and the hippies?"

"The what?"

"The hippies. You know, flower children and stuff."

"What are they?"

The old lady had always seemed so wise to me. Now, suddenly, she didn't seem to know anything. I followed up with questions about the roaring twenties, the presidential assassination, even the Gulf War. Each time, she shook her head helplessly.

Then, it dawned on me. She was just being her stubborn self. Now I was mad! Seeing my dreams of owning a dog fly off into the distance, I said in a loud irritated voice, "If you don't want to help me, just say so!"

To my surprise, she didn't return my anger, just shrugged her shoulders and said in her usual scratchy voice, "What do you want me to do, make something up?"

I sulked for a while. She was not a nice person. She was very stubborn. I knew that now. Here I'd been helping her collect plants and animals for days, and she wouldn't even help me write a stupid paper for a stupid contest. She was the meanest, orneriest person I'd ever known. But I should have known that. Who else would steal poor little plants and animals.

It was only for the sake of the plants and animals that I remained; otherwise, I would have gone home right then and there and never returned. I flung myself down by the stream and dipped my feet into the water. For a while, the two of us sat in silence.

I didn't feel like talking anymore.

CHAPTER THIRTEEN

A Pocket Full of Birds

We waited in the meadow for a long time, even longer than usual. Lounging in the warm sun was making me feel sleepy and I wanted to go home and take a nap. But there was no way—I mean, no way—I was going to leave her alone with those poor creatures.

Finally, I broke the silence. "I guess they aren't coming today," I said hopefully. "We might as well go home and try again tomorrow."

I started to get up, hoping she'd follow my lead. I should have known she wouldn't be a follower.

"Leave if you want," she said. "Nobody's keeping you. As for me, I'm staying here."

No way. I'd stay too, then. I'd show her I could be just as determined as she was. I'd just have to walk around a bit to keep myself awake, that's all.

About an hour later, she rose to her feet and picked up the cages. Instinctively, my eyes followed her's up towards the sky. Apparently, we were collecting birds today.

We followed the mother birds through the forest, this time having to look up at the sky instead of down. Sometimes, when we lagged too far behind, the adult birds would perch in a tree and beckon to us with impatient chirps. At last, they stopped in one of the trees and chirped up a storm. When we approached, they remained where they were, and the old woman quickly shinnied up the tree.

When the old lady finally came back down, the pockets of her apron were stuffed with baby birds—gangly feathered creatures that were nearly old enough to leave their nest. I watched as she tucked them in the cages. When she wasn't looking, I took some of them back out, set them on the ground, and tried to nudge them away with the toe of my shoe.

My plan didn't work at all. She knew the exact number taken from each nest, and she'd search for them until she found every last one. Not only that, most of the time the birds would come right back on their own—chirping in a whiny, complaining sort of way, kind of like they were telling on me. Stupid birds didn't know what was good for them.

The old woman never said anything about it, but I knew that she knew what I was doing. A suspicious sort of look appeared at the corner of one eye. It was a look, however, that was neither angry nor irritated. It was quite the opposite. It was as if she found the whole thing quite amusing. She seemed to be laughing inside, kind of like I do when I catch Sassy doing something sneaky. It was like she was thinking, "How stupid do you think I am?"

A sense of gloom overcame me as we carried the birds back to her house. When I set the cages on the floor, I looked down sadly at the helpless creatures, trying to beg their forgiveness with my eyes.

I lingered at her house for a while, casually checking the floor for cracks or trap doors and examining the walls for secret passageways leading to hidden rooms. I found nothing except one regular door, which opened to a small, ordinary looking bathroom. No way could all those plants and animals be hidden in there.

Every so often the old woman turned to me with that same amused expression on her face. Clearly she was enjoying my confusion. Other times, I wondered if she was simply being her usual self, and I was just seeing her differently because of my own suspicions. Still, I felt she had something over me, something she knew that I did not. It made me feel uncomfortable. I didn't know how to act.

I decided to head home. On the way back, my mind kept searching for some sort of explanation. I just couldn't figure it out. Why take the plants? Why take the animals? Why . . . where . . . how?

After dinner, I played outside with Sassy, Mick, and JayAnn. Once again, Bud failed to join us. That wasn't too unusual. At times he'd come almost every day. Sometimes it would be weeks before we'd see him again.

I felt crabby, discouraged, and very tired. I kept picturing poor Bud. I kept thinking about the old woman and the animals. Nothing was going right. I couldn't keep my mind on the games.

JayAnn started teasing me about being an old crab apple. Sassy thought it was the funniest thing she'd ever heard and started to join in. "Crab apple! Crab apple!" they'd yell every time they looked at me. Finally, I told them I was sick and went in to go to bed, even though it was still quite early.

I lay there in bed, tossing and turning, completely exhausted but unable to sleep for more than a few minutes at a time. I threw off all my covers then pulled them all back on again; I even tried sleeping with my head hanging over the edge of the mattress and the moon shining on my face. Nothing worked. Every time I closed my eyes I'd see the faces of the baby birds trapped behind the bars of the cages.

At last, in desperation, I staggered out of bed and wrenched my clothes back on. It was the middle of the night; the house was dead quiet. I plodded down the steps with my flashlight, grabbed my coat, and dragged myself up the street and across the field. Tonight, I had one advantage: I was far too tired to be even the slightest bit afraid.

When I arrived, the house looked exactly the same as the night before. Again, the thin strip of yellow light escaped through the crack at the bottom of the window, so I knew the old woman was still awake. Peeking in, I could see her sitting on the bed attending to the birds, who, still perfectly safe, flitted about their cages chirping. A trace of a smile pursed her lips and I wondered if she was thinking about all the money she'd make selling them to a laboratory. A wave of disgust coursed through me.

Leaving the window, I once more took up my watch at the base of the tree and tried to think. What could I do differently tonight that I hadn't done the night before?

I don't know how long I sat there, because, I'm ashamed to say, I fell asleep. In my dreams, I again saw the faces of the birds, squirrels, and rabbits in marvelous detail, but this time the creatures seemed at peace. Their pleasant peeps and clown-like antics seemed to be telling me they were safe and happy. Then I heard a voice inside my head softly saying, as if in a whisper, "Wake up, wake up . . . look and see for yourself . . ."

The next thing I knew I was awake, amazed at how different the dream was from the nightmares I'd had before.

I shifted my weight and discovered that my rear end was completely numb. Still pondering the odd dream, and especially the strange, shadowy voice at the end, I eased myself up and tried to walk off the numbness. The familiar pin prickles traveled up and down my legs as the circulation returned to my stiff limbs.

Then my gaze happened to shift over to the house and I noticed that, just like the night before, the light from the crack was now much brighter and whiter. The old woman had turned on all the lights. As long as I was up, I thought I might as well check to see if the birds were still in the cages. What if I was too late? Mad at myself for falling asleep, I half limped, half staggered to the window.

It ended up being the most important choice I'd ever made. What I saw changed everything. In a flash, my life was transformed.

My secure little world instantly blew apart into a million unknown possibilities.

CHAPTER FOURTEEN

People of the Light

Stooping to peer through the crack, I had no expectation of seeing anything but the room, the woman, the cages—the usual. I was completely unprepared for what I was about to witness.

The light, streaming through the crack, was white and strong, but I was almost blinded by the light inside. For a moment I saw nothing but white as my eyes watered and blinked, trying to adjust to the sudden brilliance. The whole room, the furniture, everything was as though on fire with a whiteness brighter than anything I could imagine.

I have heard people—sometimes in person, sometimes on TV—try to explain something that had happened that can't be described. They'd struggle to find the right words to match the pictures in their heads. After a while, they'd say something like, "I just can't put it into words," "I don't know how to explain it," or "You'd have to have been there to understand." Now, instantly, I knew what they meant. How do you explain something that suddenly scrambles up your comfortable understanding of what is real and what is impossible?

I will try to explain it anyway.

As my eyes adjusted, I could see that the source of the light was coming from what appeared to be a large, light-filled hole in one corner of the ceiling. Passing through the hole, the light formed a large, solid-looking beam—kind of like a high-powered searchlight or laser. It gave me the strange impression that if I could reach out and touch it, I would actually be able to feel something. At the same time, it was so transparent that I could see right through it.

The incredible beam of light seemed to have a life and energy all its own. The edges of it vibrated and pulsated rhythmically, emitting a humming noise that tickled my ears and vibrated in my throat. And the light beam was so strong that everything in the room was enveloped in a fiery glow of whiteness.

The old woman was outlined in a white halo as she walked towards the birdcages. It was then that I finally noticed she was not alone. The soft, shimmering shapes of two other people also glowed in the whiteness. One was a man, the other, a woman. Both of them looked young, probably somewhere in their twenties. And each was beautiful, more so than I ever imagined a person could be.

But it was an odd, otherworldly sort of beauty. I have always thought that, compared to most living things, people are not very good looking. But these two figures were different. Standing almost in the center of the beam, their hair shone as if highlighted with streaks of silver or gold. Loose, white, robe-like clothing draped down over their bodies. Their faces, smooth and flawless, radiated peace and happiness.

I have never seen such expressively serene faces. The closest thing I can compare them to is the wonderful look of relief when pain disappears or something horrible comes to an end. And yet, it was more than that, for it looked like a type of relief that existed without first having to experience the bad part—like not even having scars, bruises, or any reminders of *past* injuries. And it wasn't that they were perfect looking; it was simply that they looked like perfect people. The strangest part was that they weren't even smiling; and yet, I knew their happiness went way beyond anything I'd ever known. I wanted to feel the same way.

I gazed in awe as the old woman gently reached down, picked up the birds, and handed them one by one to the radiant beings. Some of the birds snuggled into the crooks of their arms; others perched on their heads or shoulders. None of them tried to escape. In fact, it was just the opposite. The birds were drawn to them, clinging like frightened children to the security of a mother. I could see why. If I'd been standing in the room, I would have run over and clung to them, too, hoping some of the emotions that shone from their faces would pass on to me.

When all the birds had been removed from their cages, the old woman and the two young people gazed back and forth at one another. Now, I don't know how I knew they were speaking, since I never saw their mouths move, but somehow I sensed the two young ones were telling the old woman that she'd done a good job. Then they told her it wouldn't be much longer— and that everybody missed her. I wasn't actually hearing any words; it was more like I felt their feelings—which said so much more than words ever could.

With amazement, I saw the two young people and the birds gradually fade from the center of the beam of light until they disappeared. It was as though the light grew thicker, less see-through, making them appear to dissolve. Before long, the powerful beam of light grew thinner, fainter, and shorter all at the same time . . . until there was nothing left of it at all.

Everything was back to normal. The old woman was still in the room. The lamp in the corner gave off its faint yellow glow—which now appeared sickly-looking and lifeless by comparison, as if it weren't really light at all. Only one thing was different: The cages were empty. And none of this, not one bit of it, fit in with the information I had stored in my head.

Too stunned to move and still trying to convince myself that what I'd seen had in fact happened, I stood blankly, staring in wonder as the old woman strolled calmly over to the kitchen as though nothing out of the ordinary had occurred.

At that point, I managed to step away from the window. I braced my forehead against the wall of the house for support and attempted to recover from the shock. I struggled to find some sense in it, some way of making the incident fit in with something I already understood. Was I still dreaming? Was I hallucinating from lack of sleep? Or—and this was by far the hardest to believe—had what I'd seen really happened?

My brain felt like it had cracked in half. I stepped to the window one more time, probably to convince myself the birds were really gone. Yes, they were gone, and now something else was, too. Try as I might, I could not see the old woman anywhere in the room.

This was too much weirdness for one night. Suddenly I felt a burst of energy and whipped around to make a mad dash for home. As I did so, I almost ran right into something—or should I say someone. There, right behind me, for who knows how long, stood the old woman, holding a plate of cookies in one hand and a pitcher of orange juice in the other. I jerked back in alarm, too afraid to feel guilty or embarrassed at being caught peeking in her window.

"Thought you might be hungry, out here for so long," she said matter-of-factly. "Thought you also might want to sit and talk a bit." Again she flashed me one of those subtle smiles that always meant so much more than her words.

How could she have known? And if she was aware that I was here tonight, did she know I'd been here the night before, too? I remembered the expression on her face when I'd met her in the field just the morning before. Yep, she definitely knew.

I must confess, I thought seriously of running, fearing she'd be furious at me for spying on her, and, even worse, for seeing something I shouldn't have seen. It only took me a moment, however, to realize how pointless that would be. After all, I knew from experience that she could easily outrun me. And, the tiny part of me that wasn't scared to death was dying for an explanation. Needless to say, all sorts of questions and weird thoughts were shooting through my brain.

I was too stunned to speak or move. Sensing this, she tucked the container of juice under the arm that held the cookies and hooked her other arm through mine. Then she led me, with surprising gentleness, around the house to the porch swing in back.

I must have managed to bend my legs, because I looked down and realized I was sitting on the swing. At first I could hardly breathe at all. Then I started breathing too much, sucking in great gulps of air like someone who'd nearly drowned.

She poured a glass of orange juice and handed it to me. I wondered, for a brief moment, if I shouldn't drink it. Perhaps she'd try to poison me for seeing what I'd seen. I wasn't, however, in a position to be choosy, so I took a sip. The old woman didn't say a word, just sat there with her steely gray eyes riveted on me. I guess she was waiting for me to calm down.

When at last I was able to speak, my words burst out accusingly, "You—you, whoever you are . . . " I stopped to take another breath. "You're stealing our stuff!"

"Nope, not stealing," came her soft-spoken reply. "Never'd do a thing like that. It's not stealing when you have permission."

"But how? Why?" I gasped.

"Here, take a cookie," she said as though we were engaged in a friendly, neighborly chat about the weather or the price of chewing gum. I couldn't believe how calm she seemed after what I'd seen. She held out the plate; I took a cookie. The food calmed me down a bit, brought me back to reality.

"Let's see . . . where to start," she said at last, raising a finger to her head and rubbing her temple as if trying to lure the memories to the surface. "First of all, I'm not from around here. You might have guessed as much by now."

I had to admit the thought had crossed my mind twenty or thirty thousand times in the last five minutes. My voice shook as I inquired, "Where are you from then?"

For an answer, she held one of her arms up to the vast night sky and moved it from side to side with a sweeping motion. "Out there in that big place you call space. So far away I couldn't even point it out to you with a high-powered telescope."

She definitely had my attention. "You're an alien from outer space?!" I asked with growing enthusiasm. As I've said before, all my life I've been mysteriously drawn to the stars. I'd always suspected, and hoped, as I stared into the night sky, that maybe, out there somewhere, someone might be looking right back at me wondering if *I* was there. Amazing! It just might be true.

She apparently found my reaction funny, since she chuckled loudly before composing herself. "I guess you could say that," she said, "though I've never thought of myself that way. I guess, if anything, I've always thought of you folks as the aliens. Besides, the way you said it made me think of myself as a little green man with two heads and six arms like on those TV shows of yours. It's not that way at all. I'm a person, just like you."

Here she paused in thought, then continued, "Or, on the other hand, maybe I should say a *little* like you, since there are certainly some big differences between my world and yours." She chuckled again. "Let's just say we're two similar people that just happen to live in two vastly different places."

Now she emitted a great, deep, throaty laugh. "Breaks me up, all the movies you people have where the aliens from outer space are savage, evil beings who attack your planet. Don't you know that superior knowledge, like space travel, comes from superior goodness? Knowledge grows from wisdom; wisdom grows from goodness. Nobody is given such vast knowledge and power unless they can be trusted with it. Furthermore, with all that advanced knowledge, why would anyone be interested in a place like this—except maybe to help out."

She turned her steely gaze on me full power. "You see, once you know you've got it really good, all that's left is the desire to help others find the same."

Ordinarily, I'd have been quite skeptical if someone told me they were an alien from outer space, but after what I'd seen, there was no doubt. If she claimed she was an alien, she was an alien. At that point, if she told me she was the Loch Ness Monster I would have believed her.

"Why didn't you tell me before?" I asked.

She smiled. "Would you have believed me?"

Definitely not; I would have thought she was utterly insane. A mad, raving lunatic who shouldn't be running around loose. There are some things you have to see with your own two eyes to believe.

"So why are you here?" I asked, my curiosity mounting.

She leaned further back into the swing and started to rock. She always seemed so patient, as if she had all the time in the world. She took in a deep breath, enjoying the fragrance of the night.

With increasing awe and wonder, I settled down—anticipating a nice long story.

CHAPTER FIFTEEN

The Mission

She quietly repeated my question before beginning her story. "Why am I here? You don't know how many times I've asked myself that question these last years. Why I ever volunteered to come to such a place as this, I mean. And to be such a person as this!" She looked down at herself and chuckled softly. I didn't understand the joke, but I would later.

She took another relaxing breath and began anew, "Well, now, the whole thing started quite a long time ago. Let me try to remember how the story goes as it's been told to me."

She paused for a minute to collect her thoughts. I kept silent.

"It seems that many years ago, on the planet where I lived, we began to hear a strange noise. In fact, I've been told that at first it wasn't as much a noise as it was a sort of vibration—like a low rumble. Nobody could figure out what it was or where it came from. At first, it was rather faint, hard to distinguish. Sometimes there were long breaks when no one could hear it much at all. Throughout the years, however, it grew louder and occurred more often until soon it could be heard quite clearly almost all the time. Then we could tell what it was. It was a groaning sound; its source was somewhere out in space. It took years of searching but eventually we discovered it was coming from a distant planet."

She stopped, turned, and looked deeply into my eyes. "Your planet," she said with a certain sadness as if hating to break the news.

"A groan?" I questioned in wonder. "Coming from our planet? I've never heard anything like that."

"That's because you're so used to it," she replied. "You've never known anything different. Your mind tunes it out, doesn't pick up on it because it's been there for as long as you can remember."

She noticed my confusion as I strained my ears to hear something. "It's a little like the way your mind tunes out the sound of a furnace running. Unless it suddenly stops or starts, you really don't pay much attention to it. You take it for granted; it just seems normal. But the inhabitants of my planet are extremely sensitive. You might say we've developed senses that go far beyond the five recognized by your world."

She paused for a sip of juice. Again I strained my ears, vainly trying to hear what I could not hear.

"Can you hear it right now?" I asked in disbelief.

"Oh my, yes!" she answered quickly. "It's almost unbearable. I've grown more accustomed to it since I've been here so long, but it's so different from what I'm used to I doubt I could ever fully tune it out no matter how long I stayed."

Eager for her to finish the story, I helped her along. "So you were out on your planet and the people there heard the noise, and then what?"

"Do you know," she replied, "how hard it is to sleep at night or go about your daily business when the sound of suffering is always there in the background haunting you? Especially when you're happy and know you've got things really good? I tell you, it's utterly unbearable!"

It made me think of Bud. How often over the past few days had I pictured him in my mind. Each time as I played on the front lawn of my wonderful house I felt an awful guilt, knowing he was living out there in a dump. I wished he had things as nice as I did. I nodded my head. I did understand that sort of feeling.

Her piercing gray eyes seemed to look deep into my soul, exploring my thoughts, searching to see if I really did know what she was talking about. She seemed convinced and nodded. "Yes, I see that you *do* understand," she said softly.

Her story continued to unfold. "After a while couldn't stand it anymore. How could we just ignore it if we could possibly help? So we sent out a search party. This, of course, was before we had discovered the origin. And you know where we ended up."

"Here," I said sadly.

She nodded her head. "The search party spoke to your planet and discovered the source of its misery."

"Wait," I interrupted. "How could they talk to the Earth?"

"There are so many different ways and forms of communicating," she replied, "which you seem to know nothing about. I guess this place has never been ready for them. Anyway, your planet was miserable because it was filled with so much unhappiness, greed, and cruelty. It was weary of witnessing countless terrible events day after day. It was tired of evil running free while good people suffered."

I was still bewildered. "What do you mean?"

"Do you really need to ask me?" *You* tell *me* what you think this place could be miserable about."

"You mean like crime, and murder, and wars, and stuff?" I answered.

She winced in apparent pain and nodded. "Those are definitely some of the worst."

She shook her head slowly as though the existence of such evils still baffled her, then added, "There are so many other things as well, both small and large. Sometimes the ones that seem small can be the worst because over time, often without realizing it, they change people in big ways. But we could sit here and think of things for hours. The list goes on and on." Her face wore a temporary mask of horror.

"Anyway," she continued, "back to the story. We, meaning the people from where I live, came up with a plan to assist your planet. We decided to give it a certain amount of time to see if the problems would self-correct. Meanwhile, we'd keep an eye on its progress and monitor the situation. So, some of our people bravely volunteered to come and live here during those years." She laughed. "I guess you could consider them spies. They simply mixed in with your people in order to observe."

With a smile on her face, she gazed off into nowhere, and I suspected she was looking back into history, remembering those bold pioneers with grand admiration. "They came," she said proudly, "with high intentions and hopes. They did countless good deeds in an attempt to improve your society. In fact, many of the good deeds your world remembers were actually performed by our people. They thought it would work wonders if they set a good example. Many of you appreciated the good deeds; some even joined in. But, sadly, things had gone too far, and the positive effects of their goodness were not enough to combat the many acts of cruelty, selfishness, and violence. You see, the situation was worse than first suspected and was rapidly going downhill. The bad actions and choices of one generation multiplied and afflicted generations to come. Each new generation started out from a lower point than the preceding one. As things got worse, distrust increased. As distrust increased, selfishness, hatred, and fear grew; and, as a result, things turned that much worse. A horrible cycle—one that continues around and around unless it's somehow broken or reversed."

Suddenly her eyes began to water. She spluttered like she was almost choking as she said, "The saddest part of all was that many of our volunteers were hurt. Some even killed—especially during times of war. Many became ill. Others suffered mentally. And there only intention was to come do something good."

She sniffled a few times and wiped her eyes, then quickly composed herself. "We had to bring them back to us." She smiled, remembering. "They were so happy to be home."

"Are you one of the spies?" I asked.

"Oh, good gracious no!" she giggled. "I was just a young thing then! But I remember seeing some of it back home."

"How could you see it?"

"Hmm," she answered. "I guess I could compare it to you watching news reports on TV. The volunteers sent reports back to the home planet to keep us informed. The information was there for anyone who was interested. Only, it happened in a different way." She tapped her head with her finger. "Think of it as having a TV program sent directly to your brain."

"Oh," I marveled. Then I wondered why I suddenly felt embarrassed. I guess her story made me feel ashamed that people on another planet were aware of all the bad things happening on ours.

She cleared her throat and continued. "Anyway, by the time the trial period was over we had a new plan. We figured the best thing to do would be to create a new planet, a new Earth—and make it as similar to this one as possible. We've been working on it ever since."

"So that's why you're taking all of that stuff?" I asked. It was getting clearer.

"That's right," she said. "There are so many good things about this place. Plants and animals that can't be found anywhere else. It would be a terrible waste to let all the good be destroyed with the bad."

"Is that where all the animals and plants went, then?" I asked. "To a new planet?"

She nodded and turned, her eyes sweeping the sky.

I was still confused—and rather sad. "But why didn't you take the mothers, too?"

"For one thing," she said, "a lot of animals don't live a long time. Many of the adult animals will probably be dead before it happens. But there's another, more important reason. The adults have lived here too long, all the while learning the wrong sorts of survival skills. Through generations, they have developed and passed along undesirable ways of thinking and coping. They know too much about fear, aggression, greed, distrust, and competition. All their natural instincts are geared to survive under wrong conditions. We can't take a chance of bringing any of those bad traits into the new world. It could cause the whole horrible process to begin anew."

Her explanation made sense. Sad as it was, I had to admit I could see her point.

"How come the mother animals took you to their babies?" I asked, remembering my surprise at their behavior.

"Oh that," she said with a hint of a nod. "That must have seemed odd to you. I sometimes forget how differently things are done here. The truth is, I sent them a message from the meadow. You might say that I called to them."

I opened my mouth to speak but she stopped me. "I know, you're going to say you didn't hear anything. It's like I told you a minute ago, there are different ways of communicating that you know nothing about. The people here are too busy trying to overcome their problems to open themselves up to anything truly new. I transmitted pictures to the minds of the animal mothers. I showed them scenes of the new planet and let them feel what it would be like to live there. Those that chose to do so led me to their babies and turned them over to my care."

I felt a thick lump form in my throat at the thought. "But how could they stand to do it—just give them up like that?"

Her answer cut me to the core. "Think about your own mother. If she knew there was a way to send you to a place where you'd only know happiness, health, and freedom, do you think she would do it? Do you think, for your sake, she would sacrifice her own feelings?"

I remembered how my mother would sit up all night with me when I was sick. Sometimes she was just as sick as I was. I thought about how she'd let Sassy and me split her dessert, pretending she didn't like it. Yes, she'd do it. It would make her miserable, but she'd do it if it was really best for us. My eyes watered; the pained expression on my face answered her question.

"You see, then," she said, "that we are not stealing. The Earth gave us permission and so did their mothers."

I paused a moment to take it all in. Then I asked, "Are you the only one doing this? Collecting all the animals and plants?"

"Gracious no!" was her reply. "I could never handle such an enormous job all by myself. There are volunteers scattered all over the planet. We've got to make sure we get samples of every species of plant, animal, and insect. We don't want anything to become extinct."

The pieces were fitting together. As her explanation started to sink in, my imagination conjured up a variety of pictures. I saw our current planet exploding into a zillion pieces or burning up in a fireball. Then another thought hit me. What about the people? What about me? The old woman had said nothing about taking along any people.

"Are you sure it's really that bad?" I asked hopefully, my voice trembling ever so slightly. "Can't it possibly change?"

She shook her head. "It is highly doubtful at this point. Many of Earth's living things are already in the process of being destroyed, just because your world is the way it is."

"But we plant new things, too," I argued. "It can't be that bad." I felt desperately panicked, as though defending my right to exist.

She again twisted her head from side to side. "You don't understand what I'm saying. It's the attitude of this world that's killing this place. It's overlooking small, important things in favor of large, unimportant ones. Let me give you an example."

She paused in thought. "Okay. Picture the middle of downtown. People walk up and down the sidewalk all day long worrying about what they consider 'important things.' If a flower was growing out of a crack in that sidewalk, struggling for life, would anybody bother to stop and move it to safety? Or would it more likely be crushed beneath someone's feet?"

The answer to the question was ridiculously obvious. "Of course no one would move it. Probably no one would even notice it at all, let alone bother to move it!" I spoke the words a little defiantly.

"On my planet," she said a bit wistfully, "it would be noticed by the first person who passed by and would be moved quickly to safety."

"You're kidding!" I gasped in disbelief. In my wildest imagination I couldn't picture it happening. What would such a planet be like?

Then I felt ashamed. My answer showed I had become hardened, self-absorbed, neglectful of the world around me. And I was sure she knew it. Still, I felt an instinctive urge to defend myself and my people, so I answered, "It seems kind of dumb to go to so much trouble over just a flower when there's so much else to worry about."

She responded softly, "What is there that is more important to worry about than a life, be it flower, animal, or person? Besides, that's just my point. Where I come from, there *isn't* anything more important to worry about. We solve the little problems so we never even come close to having big ones."

She must have seen my head drop in despair because she immediately tried to comfort me. "Now don't you feel so ashamed. It's not your fault. You've lived here all your life. You're used to your world the way it is so you can't see beyond it. It never seems to occur to anyone that just because something *is* a certain way doesn't mean that it's *right*—let alone *best*. The thought of leaving the flower in danger seems as foreign and absurd to me as moving it seems to you."

I was growing increasingly worried. At last I dared ask the question that was tormenting me most. "Won't any people be saved? Anybody at all?"

"Oh, is that what's bothering you?" she said, an answer quickly forming in her head. "Yes, of course. All the little children will be relocated when the time comes."

Realizing that by then I'd be much too old—and maybe was already—I started to shake. "I'm afraid," I blurted out. "I'm really scared. I don't want to be blown up." I put my head down in my hands.

To my surprise, she chuckled loudly. "Do you really think," she said, "that I'd be sitting here telling you this if you were going to be blown up some day?"

"You mean," I said, perking up, "that I'll get to go?"

"We'll be taking some older children," she replied, "even some adults, but not nearly as many. They will be selected with extreme care. As things become worse, the good ones will stand out even more from the bad ones, and it will be easier to make the decision between those that will be taken and those who will remain."

She tried to give me a reassuring look and added, "You have no reason to be afraid. Remember that. Try to trust."

"I'll get to go, then?" I asked again, wanting to hear a sure, solid answer.

"Yes, yes, provided all goes well, you are one of the ones we're planning to take. Besides, the planet will not be 'blown up,' as you call it. It will simply be left to itself. With the good gone—moved safely to the new planet—the evil will simply be left to run its course. Those who remain will either have to learn to cooperate and get along, or they will eventually cause their own destruction. They will find it will be much harder. Right now, whether they realize it or not, they thrive only because they have so many good, decent people to depend on and to victimize. It will be very different when only the worst remain."

I sighed with relief. I was still overwhelmed by what I'd seen and heard the last hour, but now, in a way, it was starting to sound like a great adventure.

"You see," the old woman continued, "that first day you came to the field, you didn't decide to come on your own. I called for you. Sensing your approach, I looked into your mind, found out who you were, and saw that you were mostly good—but I also felt your anger . . . anger that must be removed. I didn't want you to ruin your chance. I knew you had great potential."

I was amazed. So that's what brought me to the field that very first day. Suddenly I remembered how a strong image of the field had just popped into my mind out of nowhere.

"Just think," she said, interrupting my thoughts, "a chance to start completely over and make a new world with the help of all the best people. Picture the perfect place to live. Can you just imagine how wonderful it will be?"

As I thought about it, I realized it was really quite easy to imagine a better world, a place where you would be able to trust everyone, ask anyone for help, walk the streets alone at night without a care in the world, give any stranger a lift or invite him to dinner. The idea filled me with happiness and excitement. I wished I could go right now.

I wanted to ask the old lady thousands of other questions, but each time I tried she cut me off short.

"You're too tired to think," she insisted. "You get yourself home now and get some sleep. We'll have more time to talk tomorrow."

She walked me through the field. I was grateful for her company. Sharing her secret made me feel close to her. There was an unbreakable bond forming between us.

"By the way," she added as she saw me off down the street, "come later tomorrow. You won't be a lick of good if you're dead tired."

On the way home, a buzzing sensation filled my head. My mind was still trying to sort everything out. Strange things I'd always wondered about were beginning to explain themselves—like the existence of other beings in the universe. Now I also understood why the old woman didn't know much about our history, and why she always knew just when to meet me at the field. Either she'd somehow "called" for me or else she'd read my mind. And then there was the day I'd felt the urge to seek out the old beat-up house, the one where Bud lived. That wasn't an accident, either.

I wondered if she could read all of my thoughts or just some of them. Maybe she knew what I was thinking right now. The thought bothered me. If that were the case, I'd have no privacy. On the other hand, it was nice to know that, in spite of my thoughts, she still liked me. Furthermore, I suppose I had no right to complain about privacy after having spent two nights peeking through her window.

When I finally flopped into bed that night, I tilted my head so I could see the night sky. The stars seemed even more real than usual. No longer were they merely shiny specks on a black background. Now they seemed deeper, more meaningful—full of life!

I closed my eyes and for the first time in days no images of plants or animals tormented me.

CHAPTER SIXTEEN

Insects and Dogs

I awoke to the smell of fried bacon; sunlight flooded my room. For once, I didn't have to fight with Sassy because she and Mom had already left for the grocery store. A note taped to the refrigerator told me so. I gulped down breakfast and slid a note of my own under a refrigerator magnet telling her I was going to visit my friend again.

This time I was more anxious to see the old woman than ever. Upon reaching the field and greeting her, I found that I had gained a whole new sense of admiration and respect for her. It wasn't that *she* acted any differently; it was that I now viewed her from a whole different angle. Astounding—the person I'd once considered a crazy old lady was now a secret agent from another planet, here on an important mission.

Her manner of talking in blunt, sharp tones now seemed fascinating. Flowery words were not her style. Funny thing is, I preferred her direct way of speaking to the overly gushy talkativeness of so many other personalities. She was never rude or unpleasant, but neither did she bend over backwards to flatter or please me. Her simple language made it easy to know what to expect. She was her own kind of person.

Today, she informed me, we'd be collecting bugs. At first, I have to admit, I was a touch grossed out. I've never had much problem with your average, run-of-the-mill, garden-variety bug, but to observe so many different insects—including creepy kinds I'd never seen—swarming around in jars made me nauseous.

Sensing my mood, she asked, "What's so bad about bugs, anyway? You've just been taught to think they're creepy. Why is a fuzzy puppy cute and a fuzzy spider ugly? There's nothing about the creature itself that tells you what to think. How you react to it, all comes from right up here." She tapped me on the top of the head a couple of times with the end of a stick she was using to collect ant larvae.

Concentrating hard, I tried my best to think of the bugs as cute. It helped a little. Some of them, however, were harder to get used to than others.

As we worked, questions I hadn't asked the night before kept entering my head.

"Why do you like me to come along to help you do your collecting?" I asked. I had thought it over earlier and had concluded that I wasn't all that much help. She could have easily managed it all on her own.

"Well," she answered, "if you are one of the ones taken, some of the animals and plants will recognize you. They'll know they can trust you. It's nicer that way. Plus," she added, "it's not as much fun to work alone." She smiled at me, this time with rather a broad grin.

"Oh," I said, accepting her explanation. "Just how did you get here to our planet anyway—and those other people I saw? The two young ones?"

The well-defined wrinkles on her forehead became even more prominent. "Let's see," she said, wrinkling her forehead. "It's difficult to explain in a way you'll understand. To fully understand it involves a long process of learning, in which knowledge builds upon former knowledge. Trying to explain it properly will be a little like teaching calculus to someone who hasn't even learned to add. At best, I'll only be able to give you a basic, surface-level description of what it's really like. But I'll try."

She stopped to arrange her thoughts, then began. "In a world where there is no darkness, the power of light becomes stronger than you could ever dream possible. Even people from my world have not come close to discovering its limits. When light becomes that pure and that powerful, it makes up for trivial differences in time and space. Its speed, its capacity, becomes unlimited. To such a strong force, a small distance is about the same as a large one."

She paused again, her head tilted to one side. "Let me compare it to something you're familiar with. To a tiny child, there's a big difference between a one-pound weight and a five-pound one, but to a body builder there's hardly difference at all. Either one can be handled quite easily with very little exertion."

She looked down at the ants crawling back and forth along a path on the forest floor and added, "Or, perhaps this would be a better example. To an ant there's a huge difference between walking an inch and walking a yard. Walking a yard takes a lot more steps and energy for them. But to an adult human, the difference is minimal. A healthy adult can walk either length in a single step— virtually no time at all. It's the same way with different strengths and types of light.

She swept a string of gray hair back from her wrinkled cheek before continuing. "People on your planet believe nothing can travel faster than the speed of light, but that would be like ants believing nothing can travel faster than an ant, just because they'd never seen a person, or a horse, or a cheetah. People here have never considered that there may be different *forms* of light—just as there are different forms of *life*—kinds they know nothing about, some that are able to travel faster than others. You see, some forms of light are more pure, more concentrated. The purest, most perfect light has a speed and power that is infinite."

It made sense to me, and yet, it didn't. "I don't understand. Doesn't it ever get dark on your planet? Don't you ever have night?"

She shook her head and said, "You misunderstand me. You are talking about the physical sort of light, the part of it your eyes can see. Of course we have nighttime, but the light is still there, just as surely as the moons and stars shine in our sky. But I'm talking about the other quality of light, the one that can fill and warm a person even on the darkest night—the 'life force,' you might call it, the power of good. The outside glow of light that is visible to your eyes is only an outward symbol of what light really is. Kind of like the peel of an orange covering the real fruit inside."

Then she added, "There are a lot of uses for light and a lot of forms of light that your people have not discovered yet. They are too busy fighting over possessions to discover anything truly new. That's why most of the best discoveries are made by individuals. Usually they're outsiders—eccentrics who go in search of truth on their own. But not many people dare to step out on their own, to be their own sort of person, to think their own kind of thoughts. There is comfort in being part of a group. You never have to question whether you might be wrong because so many people are there to tell you you're right. If all the different groups would combine even just the smallest part of what they already know instead of competing against each other, they'd be amazed at what they might find."

I wanted to understand all of it better. I wondered if light could bend space . . . or was it more like a tunnel or passageway you could travel through? Or could it make an object disappear in one spot and reappear in another? I could probably think about it for years and still never truly understand. At the same time, the woman's explanation seemed strangely simple. I shook my head to clear the cobwebs from my mind.

She read my still-confused thoughts and said, "Don't feel bad that you don't understand. You really can't until circumstances are right. When they are right, it won't be something you have to think hard about. You'll *feel* it and suddenly it all will make perfect sense. It will be as though you've come from a dark room into the light of day and you'll suddenly say to yourself, 'Of course!'"

As an afterthought she added, "It's lovely when you think about it. Light, with all its glowing whiteness, appears to be the absence of color—but in truth it is a perfect combination of all colors, even shades and hues our eyes are unable to see. The spectrum of colors is infinite."

She sighed happily, pleased with her thoughts. "Pure light is the symbol for the perfect balance of all that is delightful and beautiful."

A thrill of electric excitement charged up my spine. Traveling through light to a new planet. What would it feel like?

Then came a question I feared to ask. "Who else will be going? You said there'd be others besides the young children. Who else will go when the time comes?"

She turned towards me but said nothing, inviting me to think it out for myself. I searched my mind for who else might be taken. Then it hit me like a lightening bolt. Like she'd said, I didn't *think* it, I *felt* it.

"Bud! Bud will go too, won't he!"

Her face glowed with approval. "Yes," she said. "Bud is one of the sure things. Anyone who can create good in the middle of so much bad can be trusted with anything. He's so genuine. It's too bad there aren't more like him."

"His house and parents are awful," I said, my face drawn into a sympathetic grimace.

She turned to hand me a very small grasshopper and said, "In some cases, it seems to be a great injustice that you don't get to choose who your parents will be. Kind of get stuck with what you've got, don't you? Still, his parents have had their troubles, too. They weren't always like that. They were once little children, full of delight and hope. People change, you see, often becoming more desperate, less hopeful as they grow older and unexpected disappointments and tragedies occur. There may come a day when you'll feel that way too."

She paused for a moment, apparently not sure she should have said so much. As she looked at me, a wave of sympathy shadowed her face. I was puzzled by the sudden change. A second or two passed before she looked like her old self again.

"In Bud's case, however, he turned a bad situation into a strength. It has made him strong and sensitive at the same time, two qualities you don't often find together."

"What about Mick and JayAnn?" I asked.

She shook her head in disappointment. "JayAnn's definitely headed the wrong way. She knows what she wants and will do anything it takes to get it—even if she has to rip it right out of another person's hands." She chuckled, and I knew she was referring to the garden hose episode. "Unfortunately," she continued, "JayAnn's always wondering what's in it for her. She's a competitor, not a cooperator. People like that aren't good for the new place."

It made me sad. I wondered if there was anything I could do that would help.

The old woman, sensing my sadness, said, "I know. She doesn't seem that bad yet. Few people do when they are children. But you'll be amazed at what can happen when a person like her gets older and her chances for influence and power increase. Still, you never know. People are rather unpredictable creatures. They are greatly influenced by other people, events, and circumstances. Who knows, maybe you can help her. Maybe, in some strange way, you already have."

"And Mick?" I asked.

She shrugged. "Still could go either way. Trouble is, he bows down to JayAnn so much—follows her around and lets her tell him what to do. He needs to learn to think for himself and make his own choices—even if it's hard."

My thoughts were interrupted by a flash of panic. What about Sassy? We'd never talked about my little sister, but somehow I was sure the old lady would know all about her.

"What about Sassy?" I asked casually, pretending it didn't really matter to me. She was annoying, but I was used to her—I didn't want her left behind.

She shrugged her shoulders again and answered, "She's too little now. No one knows. A great portion of her fate might rest in your hands. I know she's difficult for you to handle, but stop for once and consider why."

With guilt, I already knew the answer. All she wants is my attention, a little of my time and approval. She just doesn't know any of the right ways of getting it. Most of all, she wants to be big like me.

"You see," the old woman interjected, "everyone is so interconnected. One person's chance for success often depends on the actions and decisions of countless others. That's why you can never have a truly magnificent planet unless everyone's willing to make it that way. It's lack of trust that ruins it every time. That and selfish greed."

I didn't ask any more questions. I already had plenty to think about.

For the rest of the day, as we worked, I kept feeling guilty about how I'd treated Sassy. It was hard for me to keep my mind on my work. Every weird little bug's face reminded me of her—the resemblance was astounding! As I scooped larvae out of an anthill, I tried to figure out what I could do to make things better.

Awhile later, the old woman's throaty voice broke the silence. "Well, well!" she said cheerfully. "Who do we have here?"

Turning to look, I immediately flew to the old woman's side. She was holding a fuzzy, gray puppy on her lap. I dropped everything in my excitement.

The tiny pup was round and plump, with small paws. I could tell he wouldn't grow to be very big. Obviously a mutt, he was probably the runt of the litter. He wriggled his hind-end and reached up playfully with his snout, trying to lick the old woman's wrinkles. She gave him a pat on the head and laughed.

Then, to my overwhelming delight, she held the puppy out to me and said, "I believe this belongs to you."

I was confused, stunned, overjoyed all at the same time. Then my heart sank. "I can't just take him," I said miserably. "I'm sure he belongs to someone else."

"He doesn't," the old woman insisted. "Someone dropped him off at the edge of the field earlier today— an inexcusable way of riding oneself of too many puppies without taking the responsibility of finding them good homes." A look of anguish spread across her face. "Since then, the poor thing's been wandering around lonely, hungry, and afraid."

"How do you know?" I asked, forgetting for a moment who it was I was talking to.

"I know," was all she said.

I believed her. I swept him up into my arms and cradled him tightly while petting his soft head. Forgetting all about the bugs, I plopped down on the forest floor to play with him. After a moment, a thought occurred to me.

"You called him to come to us, didn't you?"

She reached over, stroked the dog under the chin, and said, "I knew he needed you, that's all. I just told him there was someone here who wanted a dog really badly. I figured you two were a perfect match."

She tried to shrug it off, but I could see her eyes shining between folds of wrinkled skin. It made her feel pleased to know that she'd made me happy—and the dog, too. She took a piece of rope and tied it loosely around the pup's neck to form a makeshift leash.

"Look," she said, once again reading my mind, "it's late afternoon and I can handle the rest myself. You had a hard night last night. Why don't you take him home so he can get used to his new place."

At the mention of home, a scary thought hit me. "What if Mom won't let me keep him?" I said, fearing the worst.

Sparkles danced in the old woman's eyes as she said, "She will."

I jumped to my feet and surprised myself by giving her a hug. I couldn't help it; I was too happy.

The old woman's face beamed with delight. "Oh, stop making such a big fuss," she said, handing me the leash.

I turned and raced off through the meadow, the pup chasing my heels. Then, I thought about Sassy, stopped in my tracks, spun around, and ran back.

"Umm," I said awkwardly, "I'll still come and help you . . . but I might not always be able to stay for so long."

"I understand," she said, smiling. I knew she was reading my mind again and approved of my thoughts.

At home, Mom was outside watering a dry spot in the lawn. Seeing the dog at my feet, she threw me a disapproving glare, but after I explained to her how he had just been dumped off in the fields, her face softened and she agreed to let me keep him. She even stooped to give him a few quick pats.

"Well, he does seem like a real nice little dog," she said. "And I'll have to admit I'll feel better about you running off by yourself all the time like you do if you have a dog along for protection."

My eyes dropped down to the tiny ball of fur by my feet. Didn't look like he'd be a whole lot of protection to me—but I wasn't about to argue.

"Where's Sassy?" I asked.

"She fell asleep watching cartoons and I put her on her bed," Mom answered.

I made my way down the hall and into Sassy's room. There she was, lying all alone on her big bed looking very small and lonely. Then I did something I've never done before, maybe because I was so happy about the pup. I scooped her up and hugged her. She woke up.

"What are you doing!" she said, jerking back in surprise when she saw it was me.

"Sassy, just look at my new friend!" I screamed. Overwhelmed with joy, I lifted the gray pup and put him on her lap. I wanted her to be as excited as I was.

Sassy squealed with delight, then giggled as the pup's slimy, rough, wet tongue tickled her hand. He chewed on her fingers, then bounced up to lick her right smack on the lips.

"Where'd ya get him?" she grinned, hardly able to contain her happiness.

I related the whole story. Not the part about the old woman, of course, but the same story I'd told Mom about him being dumped off in the field.

When I was done telling the story, I added, "Hey, Sass, want to go hike up the hill and watch the stars come out after dinner? Just you, me, and the dog?"

"Not JayAnn and Mick?" she asked suspiciously.

"Nope, just us."

Her eyes glowed and she nodded her head vigorously.

"It will be our own adventure," I said. "We'll take our flashlights and pack some snacks."

Her eyes grew wider and she began to jump wildly up and down on her bed.

It was as we were heading up the hill that night that I finally started to see things differently. Sassy had always been so much younger than me that I'd never really known what to do with her. All my life she'd seemed like a nuisance, a pest, a major source of irritation. Now I could picture us growing up as best friends. After all, if I could be friends with someone a lot older than me, why not with someone a lot younger?

Strangely, it suddenly was not all that hard to imagine.

CHAPTER SEVENTEEN

Flower in the Crack

I named my pup Star. It wasn't the most original name in the world, but it was the only one that seemed to make sense. Nobody knew how I'd come to pick the name, and of course I couldn't tell anyone. I wanted his name to remind me of the person who'd brought him to me. Since I couldn't name the dog "Old Lady," Star was the best alternative. It reminded me that there were other people living on other planets way out among the stars.

The first thing I needed to do, after eating breakfast the next morning, was to pick up some supplies for my dog. I figured I had just enough money left in my savings to buy a collar, a dish, and a bag of dog food.

"Sassy!" I called over my shoulder into the other room. She scurried in at lightening speed. Ever since our adventure to the hill the night before, she'd been surprisingly agreeable, even eager to please me. She stood in front of me, huffing and puffing, waiting expectantly. This was starting to get fun.

"I need you to do something very important for me," I said, using my most serious voice. "It's something I am trusting you to do and no one else but you. Do you think you can handle it?"

Her eyes widened and she nodded her head eagerly. "Yeah! I can do it for sure!"

"Okay, then," I said. "I need you to take care of Star for me while I go somewhere. You'll have to make sure he doesn't run out in the street or get lost. Did you get all that?"

She nodded again and blurted out, "What should I do with him?"

"You could take him on a walk around the yard," I suggested. "Why don't you introduce him to your plants or something."

Sassy had a strange way about her—actually, she had *a lot* of strange ways about her. She'd spend hours outside talking to trees or bushes. I guess because they were good listeners and couldn't get away.

"Now," I continued, "you've got to make sure he doesn't choke on his rope. You know, like I showed you yesterday. If he yelps, it means he doesn't like what you're doing. Think you can handle it all by yourself?"

"Yes, I will, I will," she said impatiently, taking Star's rope from my hand. "Get over here, doggy. You have to do what *I* say now."

I knew, when I asked, that Sassy would jump at the chance to be in charge of anything. At last there was someone smaller she could boss around who might actually obey her orders. I wondered if I was making a mistake leaving Star in the hands of such a ruthless dictator.

"You have to call him 'Star,' Sassy, not 'doggy,' or he'll never learn his name," I told her.

"Awright," she said, tugging on the rope. "Come on, then, Star."

I could hear her singing a little song she'd made up as she led him around the corner. "Star, Star, Star, your name's Star, Star in the sky, shooting Star . . ."

Her voice faded as she pulled him outside.

I got my things together. Before leaving for the store, I went to the window like a nervous parent to see how things were going. I could see Sassy's mouth moving nonstop. Apparently, she was getting after Star because his feet were muddy. Then she started giving him a detailed tour of our backyard, telling him exactly where he could and could not go and what he could and could not do there. She'd be a merciless mother some day.

I pedaled my bike to the pet store near the edge of town. I'd been there so many times before that the owner knew me by sight. This time, I surprised him by marching right past the puppies in the display case.

Mr. Samuelson was delighted to hear about my new pup. He helped me pick out a bright red collar, a dog

161

dish, and some puppy food. I didn't have enough money for a leash, so I'd have to get by with the rope for a while.

As Mr. Samuelson handed me the bag, I saw him sneak in a handful of dog biscuits and a few rawhide chew bones. I've always liked him. People who really like dogs always seem to be extra nice.

I was about to hop on my bike and head for home when something the old woman had said popped into my mind. I hid my sack behind a bush so nobody would steal it. That way, I wouldn't have to carry it with me. (Funny thing is, it doesn't matter what's in the sack, if you leave it out in public, chances are someone will come along and swipe it. It could be a bag full of smelly garbage, and when you came back for it, it would be gone.)

I know I shouldn't have done it, since it's more dangerous there, but I rode down to a busier part of town, got off of my bike, and walked up and down the sidewalk, looking and looking. At first I saw nothing. Well, nothing except hordes of people and rows of cars. I marveled at how much dirtier the city seemed and how much weirder looking some of the people were than the last time I'd been there with Mom and Dad. But, who knows? Maybe some of the normal-looking people were more dangerous than the strange ones.

For a moment, I felt kind of scared and alone. Then, I went right back to my business, figuring that if I didn't bother anyone, they probably wouldn't bother me. I walked along for several blocks, concentrating on the cracks in the sidewalk. Still, I saw nothing.

I was about to give up when I had one last idea. Choosing one of the cracks, I got down on my stomach and stretched out lengthwise on the cement next to it. People had to step around me as they hurried past. I'll bet some of them gave me some odd looks, but I can't be sure since I never looked up.

That's when I finally found what I was looking for: one tiny flower, its face barely peeking out over the top of the crack. When I say tiny, I mean tiny. The whole flower, petals and all, was only about a fourth the size of the fingernail on my pinky. But it was definitely a flower, with everything a large flower has: a fuzzy yellow center, a circle of oval, pink petals, a slender, thread-like stem, and a splash of green leaves.

I wondered why such a tiny thing would bother to grow when no one would notice it. "What a waste," I remember thinking. Then I realized how wrong I was. So wrong. As if the only reason for a flower to grow was to please a person! Perhaps some little ant or spider passed by every day and it made them stop for a moment and smile. Or maybe the flower just enjoyed being alive.

I was worried about the flower. I felt sorry for it.

I slid over until my head hung down into the gutter by the street, where I found the remnants of an old, crumpled paper cup with the name of the hamburger shop down the street printed on its side. Someone had tossed it carelessly into the street—even though a garbage can stood only three feet away. Turning the cup upside down, I placed it over the flower to protect it from being crushed while I was gone.

I hurried back to my bike, retrieved my sack, and pedaled home as fast as I could. Rummaging through our garage, I came across a large clay flowerpot and filled it with dirt from the garden. Then I stuffed it in a plastic bag with my "spatula" tool and slipped the straps of the bag over my bike's handlebars.

From around the corner of the backyard I could hear Sassy's voice droning on, giving my dog orders. Things seemed to be going okay with the two of them, so I straddled my bike and hurried back to town.

It took me a while to find the crack with the flower. Someone must have kicked the cup back into the gutter. As carefully as I could, I dug up as much of the flower's roots as possible and tucked it into the pot. I knew exactly where this flower was going—to a place where even the tiniest flower would be important.

Returning home, I hid the pot in a corner of the garage. I sighed with relief. It felt good to be back home, away from the city.

I went around back to look for Sassy and Star. Sassy seemed disappointed to see me. There was something about her face that made her look guilty. I glanced down at the ground and noticed some of her old doll clothes near her feet. If I'd been gone much longer I would have returned to find my dog in a dress with matching hat and high heels.

"Saaaaaaassy," I said, drawing out her name with a grumble in my voice. "Star wouldn't have liked that."

While attempting to look innocent, she tried to stuff the doll clothes under a bush with the back of her foot. She doesn't think I'm very smart.

"Like what?" she asked. "All I did was take really good care of him. I even washed the mud off of his paws."

"You know what I'm talking about," I grumbled. "If I'm gonna leave Star with you, I've got to know you can be trusted."

"I can, I can. I promise," she replied nervously, her eyes pleading and her face wrenched in panic. "I won't ever dress him up again. I just didn't know, is all."

"W-e-e-l-l-l-l-l . . . " I said, drawing the word out longer than necessary to leave Sassy in a worried state of suspense. "I guess I'll give you one more chance. But one, and only one."

Sassy let out her breath in relief. She pulled the puppy close with smug satisfaction. "Look at how Star loves me so much," she said. Meanwhile, Star was gnawing on her fingers, struggling to get away.

"Yeah, sure," I said. "Whatever you say."

Reaching into my sack, I took out the new red collar, the bowl, the food, and the treats. Star had to sniff each one of them separately before giving a yelp of approval.

It was difficult to get the collar around his neck. He kept gripping one of the ends in his teeth and wouldn't let go. I think he wanted to play tug-o-war. I was glad to have Sassy's help. She held his head while I pried his mouth open and pulled the collar out. Then she clamped his mouth shut while I buckled it around his scrawny neck.

Once I got the collar on, I picked him up and squeezed him. Now he really seemed like my dog. I couldn't believe I was actually sitting there holding *my dog*!

For about an hour Sassy and I played with him in the yard. Then he suddenly got tired and collapsed in a fuzzy little ball to warm himself in the sun. We stroked his fur gently as he slept.

We've got to be careful not to maul the dog too much," I told Sassy. "Otherwise he could get sick and die."

"What does that mean?" Sassy inquired.

"I don't know," I answered truthfully. "But I always hear grownups say that to kids."

After a few minutes, I started to worry. It was now late afternoon and I hadn't been to see the old lady. I was dying to go, but I knew Sassy would definitely try to follow. How could I tell her she couldn't come—especially after she'd been so good all day? "Good,"that is, for Sassy. I guess she couldn't help being at least a little bad. Mostly, I didn't know if the old woman would approve of me bringing her. I also wasn't sure I wanted

Sassy to know about my new friend. Sassy is such a blabbermouth.

Luckily, Mom came out before too long and, seeing what a mess Sassy was, marched her right inside for a bath. Sassy kicked and screamed the entire time, yelling over and over that she wanted to stay with me and Star.

The second she was safely inside, I sped to the garage and grabbed the flowerpot, stuck it in the plastic bag, and slung it over the handlebars. Star was still quite sleepy, so I put my jacket on, zipped it half way up, and put Star inside—leaving his head barely sticking out over the top of the zipper so he could see out.

Then the two of us hurried off to find the old woman.

CHAPTER EIGHTEEN

Flower for a Friend

This time she wasn't waiting in the field when I arrived. I was wondering what to do next when a clear picture of the meadow flashed into my mind. I knew she was there.

When I reached the meadow, she was lounging in the sun, waiting, not the slightest bit surprised to see me. This time I knew why.

"Well," she said, propping herself up on her elbows. "I see you brought Star with you. Good."

I hadn't told her what I'd named the pup yet, but I wasn't surprised to learn she already knew. Anyone who could send messages to animals could certainly find out something as simple as that. Perhaps she'd called to Star this morning and asked him his name. I was curious.

"How'd you know I named him Star?" I asked.

"Why, because that's his name, of course," she said with a twinkle in her eye.

"But I didn't think of the name until just this morning."

"What makes *you* think *you* came up with the name? Star must have told it to you. That was the name he wanted. He told me yesterday that his name was Star," she replied, relishing the look of awe on my face.

The thought of it amazed me. Had Star somehow put the name into my head instead of me coming up with it on my own? Where do ideas and thoughts really come from, anyway? I had once believed it had been my idea to come to the field on the day I'd met the old woman. Now I knew better. How many other ideas of mine had really come from somewhere else without my knowing? I shook my head hard so my mind would clear.

"What's that you've got there in your other hand?" she asked.

"Oh, yeah, I brought you something," I said, holding out the flowerpot. "I found this squished in a crack near the city. Maybe you could send it to the new planet where it will be safe."

My eyes rested on the tiny pink blossom, its head raised on its half-inch-long neck in the center of the huge pot. It was almost invisible. It looked like a pink speck in the middle of a vast wasteland of dirt.

"Well," she said, chuckling, "it will certainly have room to grow in there! I don't believe I've got one like that yet. Must've been on someone else's list. Bring it here." She looked closer. "No, I'm sure I don't have one of those."

"It's awful small," I said, embarrassed.

"Small things can often be the best," she replied. "They are true treasures, since most people never even know they exist. Cute little thing. I'm glad you brought it to me. I think I'll plant it myself." Then she added, "Somewhere safe, of course, where nothing will squash it by mistake."

"You mean, you sometimes get to go to the new planet?" I inquired.

She shook her head. "Nope. I haven't been there yet, but I'll get to go soon."

"How do you know what it's like then?"

"Oh, I've heard all about it for years," she said. "And sometimes they send me pictures." She tapped her head. "That way I can see how it's coming along."

I figured she must be referring to the people who were working on the new planet. I was glad to know she would take my flower there personally. I wouldn't want it to be lost.

"Maybe the ants and spiders will like it," I suggested.

The corners of her mouth drew upward into a gentle smile. She took the pot from me and placed it safely on the ground next to her.

"I meant to come a lot earlier today," I said apologetically.

"Oh?" was her simple reply.

"Yeah," I said. "But I couldn't get rid of Sassy. She'd try to follow me for sure."

"So why didn't you bring her along?" she asked.

Her reply surprised me. "You mean I can? I didn't know if I could."

"Why, sure," she said. "I don't try to stop anyone from doing whatever they feel is right."

"I thought, though, that she might blab everything."

"She doesn't have to know *everything*," she suggested. "You didn't for a long time."

That's true, I thought. "But she'll see you and maybe tell Mick and JayAnn where I go. Somehow, I don't want them here. I don't mind much if Sassy comes, or Bud too, but I don't want the others here." I wondered what it was that made me feel that way.

"Won't matter at all in a day or two anyway," she said with a wistful sigh. "Guess I might as well tell you. In a day or two I'll be gone."

I felt a lump form in my throat. "You're going away?" I asked.

"Yes," she answered.

"When will you be back?" For some reason, I dreaded her answer. Maybe because I knew what it would be.

She shrugged her shoulders. "Who knows. Probably never."

With an ache in my voice, I asked, "Why do you have to leave so soon?"

She chuckled again. "I've been here a very long time. You just didn't know me until recently. You've passed me in the stores and on the streets many times without even noticing. After all, most people don't pay much attention to an ordinary, little old lady."

Her smile widened as she continued, "You see, I've nearly collected all the creatures and plants on my list. In fact, tomorrow's my last day. I've got some more birds to collect today, then tomorrow a batch of mice. After that, there's no reason for me to stay any longer."

"They'll make you go?" I asked.

"I want to go."

"But why?" I pleaded. I didn't want her to leave.

Her eyes met mine. "This isn't my home. I've been gone such a very long time. I'm just dying to go back."

"Are you homesick?" I asked.

"Very," she whispered.

"I know what that's like." I was thinking back to the summer I'd spent visiting my grandparents in another state. "I've been homesick, too."

"If you ever came to my planet," the old lady said, looking deep into my eyes, "you'd never be homesick for yours again."

"What's it like?" I asked.

"Oh, it's so wonderful!" Her eyes lit up at the thought. "It's so different from this place in countless ways . . . and yet, a little like it in others."

"And the people there are nice?"

"Oh, yes!" she answered, her index finger stroking the edge of the pot that held my pink flower. "That is the greatest difference between here and there. On my planet, everyone's nice. Nobody has any reason or desire not to be. Absolutely everyone can be trusted. It's mainly because of the people and creatures that live there that the whole place is aglow with such brilliant light. I tell you, it's more wonderful than you could ever believe!"

Her eyes glowed, lit by some internal fire. I thought it odd that her eyes could look so young and yet be stuck on such an old body.

Then, she added, "When I first came here, I felt like I'd gone from a beautiful dream to a horrible nightmare. I wasn't sure if I could handle it, but I'm glad I did. I'll always remember this as a daring adventure. It's made me stronger. It's made me appreciate home even more."

For a moment, I tried to picture her planet. "You know what?" I said at last.

"What?"

"I think I'm homesick for your planet, too."

She didn't know what to say, just looked at me with pity. She seemed a little choked up. I thought I heard her whisper to herself under her breath, "If you only knew . . . if you only knew."

She quickly changed the subject. "There are the birds now. Want to come with me to get them?"

I was already on my feet. "Sure," I said. Then I hesitated. "What about Star?" I asked. "Won't he scare them?"

"Oh goodness no!" she said. "I'll tell him not to."

Later that day, after I had helped her carry the cages to her house, I presented her with another series of questions.

"Will you be working in the meadow tomorrow to gather the mice?"

"Yes," she said.

"Then later on they'll come and get you and take you away?"

"Yes," she said again.

"The same way?"

"The same way."

"Will it be at night again?"

"Yes, at night, I believe."

I hesitated for a moment, shifting my weight awkwardly from one foot to the other. I knew what I wanted to ask next, but I didn't dare.

She turned, her eyes riveted on me in a searching sort of way. Then, without my saying a word, she said, "Yes, you can come see me off if you'd like."

A peculiar feeling ran through me—to know she could read my thoughts like that. "What time should I come?" I asked.

She smiled and said, "You'll know when it's time. I promise."

Heartache followed me as I left her house that day. I was almost to the trees at the edge of the field when she called after me, "Don't forget to bring Sassy tomorrow. But only for the day."

I understood.

I let Star off his leash, and he and I raced each other through the field. He nipped at my toes and heels as I ran, madly trying to catch my shoelaces in his teeth. Now that the old lady was going away, I was extra glad to have Star around. Funny, I hadn't even known her all that long, but she seemed so important to me. At least I'd have Star to remind me of her.

By the time I got home, dark clouds were knitting themselves together and the sky above them was turning from blue to smoky gray. A flicker of lightening flashed in the distance. Star whined a bit in fear, then tried to dig a hole in the cement. I guess his ears could hear the distant thunder.

I was thrilled to see the thunderstorm building. It would be one of those quick summer downpours that cools everything off, then just as suddenly disappears. With any luck, the storm would pass and there would be plenty of time to "Explore the Nile" after dinner.

It seemed like a long time had passed since the last hard rainstorm. It was the day I'd met the old woman. So much had happened since then. It seemed like forever. I felt like a different person.

Sure enough, less than half an hour after dinner the sky began to show signs of clearing.

"Run out and get my treasure box, will you, Sassy?" I yelled. She whizzed off in a blur.

When she came back, she peered over my shoulder as I inspected the treasures inside.

"You know what, Sass?" I announced when I was finished, "I think you should start a treasure box of your own."

"Really?" Her eyes brightened. I could tell she was thrilled with the idea.

"After we explore the Nile, I'll help you make one before you go to bed," I offered.

"Goody! Goody! Goody!" she repeated over and over as she jumped up and down behind me. "I'm gonna go tell Mom I get a box!" She skipped out of the room.

"You'll have to find your own treasure, though," I yelled after her.

I inched over to the window and waited for the last drops of rain to fall.

CHAPTER NINETEEN

Sassy's Box

As soon as the rain had cleared, Sassy, Star, and I were standing at the curb. Since we were the first ones there, we got first dibs on places. I'd found one of Mom's garden tools for Sassy to dig with, and she was clutching it tightly in both hands, a big grin etched across her face.

A few minutes later, Mick and JayAnn came bounding out their front door. Earlier, Sassy told me that while I'd been gone the two of them had heard Star barking and had come over to see him. She said JayAnn had been so jealous of my pup, even though she pretended not to like him very much. (Even Sassy had JayAnn figured out.)

"Hi, Star," Mick said, stooping down to pet my pup.

JayAnn rushed right past as if she couldn't be bothered and hurried toward the gutter to beat Mick for choice of spots. She happened to pick the spot next to me—wouldn't you know it, the very one Sassy had claimed. I saw Sassy's face fall.

"You can't go there, JayAnn," I told her.

"Can too!" she sneered. "You've already got your place."

"That's Sassy's spot," I hissed.

She threw Sassy a dirty look. I saw Sassy cringe. "Sassy doesn't get a spot!" she said in a snobbish tone that was even more sharp and snappy than usual.

"She does *too*," I said firmly. "She got here first, so she gets that spot. That's the rules—in case you forgot." I tried to match JayAnn sneer for sneer, but knew I wasn't anywhere in her league.

JayAnn thought quickly. "She's your little sister, so she has to share with you."

I thought quicker. She would not win this time, not when Sassy was so excited. "In that case," I answered back, "you have to share with Mick, since you're *his* little sister."

Her glare could have turned water to stone. She stuck her nose in the air and announced, "I don't like that spot any more anyway. It's too close to you." Pinching her nose between two fingers, she stomped off down to the other end. Once again managing to have the last word, she added, "Sassy's too little to do it anyway."

Sassy stood there in absolute awe and gratitude that I'd defended her spot for her. She sidled up closer to me, probably for protection. At home, Sassy was as feisty and ornery as can be, but when it comes to JayAnn, she knows she's met her match. Sassy was suddenly timid.

We all waited a while longer for Bud to show. I began to worry. No one else seemed a bit concerned. (Of course, they didn't know what I knew.)

Squirming impatiently, Sassy kept nudging me and asking, "Can we start yet?" She was starting to get on my nerves again. I couldn't blame her, though. After all, this was her first time. She was bound to be excited.

Then Bud came into view, far up at the end of the street, clomping along toward us as fast as he could go in his clumsy, joyful sort of way. A sigh of relief escaped my lips.

When he reached us, everyone clamored around him to check out his new treasure box. Mick was completely in awe of it; as expected, JayAnn's nostrils flared with envy.

I was looking at something different, something no one else seemed to notice—nor would they have thought much about it if they had. Traces of old bruise marks covered his arm and ran up the side of his neck to his face. Most of them were faint and yellow-looking, hardly showing up at all. A few places, however, were still black and blue.

I cringed at the sight. A sick feeling gnawed at my stomach. I was pretty sure I knew where those bruises had come from. In my mind, I pictured the sloppy, mean-looking man in the ragged undershirt. I shuddered.

Bud, on the other hand, was grinning his usual toothy grin, acting as always, as if he didn't have a care in the world. I couldn't figure out how he could be the way he was. I finally understood why he would be perfect for the old woman's new world.

I must admit—with guilt—that I thoroughly enjoyed seeing JayAnn seethe with jealousy over Bud's new box. I wanted Bud to have something worthy of envy. I knew JayAnn was jealous on the inside, even though outwardly she pretended that Bud's box wasn't as good as hers. Then, after a while, she graciously offered to trade him, if he wanted, since she was getting rather bored with hers.

Bud good-naturedly shrugged his shoulders and said, sure, he'd trade with her if she really wanted. Mick's jaw dropped in amazement. I jumped in to stop him; I couldn't let this happen.

"No way, Bud," I said, much to JayAnn's disgust. "Tell her 'no way.' JayAnn's isn't near as good as yours and she knows it. Plus, it has your name written on it." I ran my finger along the lettering. "Don't you like yours best?" (I also should have mentioned how ridiculous it would be for Bud to own a treasure box covered with flowers, but the thought hadn't occurred to me.)

"Yeah, I guess so," Bud said sheepishly.

"Well, why in the world would you want to trade her then?"

He shrugged off the question as though the whole thing didn't really matter much. "I don't know. I guess because she wants me to."

Leaning over to admire the smooth wood, I insisted, "Well, you can't." That's her box and this one's yours forever, okay?"

He shrugged once more. "All right," he said.

I guess when you're used to having nothing, things like treasure boxes aren't as big a deal to you as they are to other people. Bud seemed to really like the box, but I had the feeling he could get by just as well with his old tin can.

JayAnn shot me a scowl so fierce I was sure she wanted to tear my brains out right then and there. I couldn't help stepping back a little. Then, furious, she mouthed the words, "Mind your own business."

Luckily, at that moment, Sassy, who couldn't stand to wait a second longer, yelled out, "GO!"

We all flew to our places and began digging.

This time I wasn't so lucky. All I found was a bent sucker stick and a leaf skeleton that looked neat but fell apart when I tried to scrape it off.

Working next to me, Sassy was becoming frustrated. Digging with all her might, clumps of mud were flying everywhere, but she wasn't finding anything. Star was trying to help her by frolicking back and forth through the mud, biting at her shovel, and barking.

I felt sorry for her. She just wasn't very good at it. It took patience and skill, two qualities Sassy wasn't that big on. Slipping my hand into my front pocket, I felt around until I found some lose change. I pulled out a dime.

"Sassy," I called out, "pull Star out of your way so you can work better."

The second she turned to push him away, I reached over and patted the dime deep into the mud, slicking a layer of silt over it with the side of my hand.

"Try over in this area, Sassy," I said, pointing in the general area of the hidden coin. She worked and worked, but kept missing it.

I tried again. "How about right between here and there," I suggested, drawing a box in the mud to narrow the area down to a three or four inch square. Still, she kept missing it, flinging mud this way and that in some kind of wild frenzy.

I tried one last time. "How about right here in this exact spot." I plunked a mucky finger on the precise location of the dime. "And slow down a bit," I added as an afterthought.

Seconds later, "EUREKA!" she shrieked with delight, holding up the dime.

I tried to act surprised. "Wow, Sassy! You found a big chunk of genuine silver!"

She glowed with pride, never even suspecting the part I had played. Fortunately, the others had also been too busy to notice.

When we finished with the excavating, I helped Sassy wash and polish her dime. Then I kept my promise: We went in to make Sassy her very own treasure chest.

"I want it with tons of diamonds and jewels and rubies and sparklies all over the lid," she babbled as I cut out pieces of colored construction paper.

Not having the slightest idea how to create valuable gems out of construction paper, I thought fast and said, "You be in charge of making that part, Sass."

When we finally finished taping the lid to the base, she proudly took it out to show Mom and Dad. Blobs of balled-up paper were glued in thick clumps all over the top. Sassy lined the inside with a thick layer of cotton, then laid the dime gently on top, a rare, fragile artifact resting on a velvet cushion. No dime had ever had it so good.

Later that night, as I was climbing into bed, Mom appeared at my doorway. One of her hands was covering her mouth in an attempt to keep from laughing. She motioned to me with the other.

I followed her down the hallway to Sassy's room. We both stuck our heads around the corner and peeked inside.

Sassy was sound asleep in bed, one arm wrapped tightly around her treasure box, the other clutching a toy gun. The cover of her night-light had been tipped so that a beam of light rested directly on the box.

Mom and I stifled our giggles as we crept back from the doorway. "I tried to get her to keep it under her bed like you do," Mom whispered to me between fits of laughter, "but she'd have none of it. She said she was too afraid a robber might come in and steal it."

The thought of a burglar breaking into our house just to steal Sassy's glue-streaked, clumpy-looking treasure box made me laugh even harder.

"What's the gun for?" I managed to ask, choking on my laughter.

Mom, tears running down her cheeks, gasped out, "To shoot any pirates who might happen to come along."

At that, the two of us raced down the hall to my room, closed the door, and laughed our heads off. My eyes watered and my stomach muscles hurt so badly that I nearly threw up. It felt good to laugh that hard. I could tell Mom thought so, too. Maybe Sassy would be a comedian when she grew up.

Star, who had followed us down the hall, was working himself into a frenzy trying to lick our faces. He seemed upset that he hadn't been let in on the joke.

"I can see why Sassy was worried," I said once I'd gained control. "We have *so* many pirates wandering around our neighborhood."

The two of us broke out into another fit of laughter.

Finally we calmed down. Both of us were sprawled across the bed, holding our stomachs. "You've been real good to Sassy lately," Mom said to me as she pushed a strand of hair back from my face. "It really means a lot to her. I've never seen her so delighted as when she came home from your hike up to the hill the other night."

"Maybe I'll take her with me tomorrow, too," I said, as if the idea had just come to me. Actually, I'd been planning on it ever since I'd seen the old lady earlier that day.

"That would be nice," Mom said. "For me, too," she added with a sigh.

She closed the door part way as she left so the light down the hall wouldn't keep me awake. Star cuddled up next to me on the bed. I loved Star; he was just the right sort of dog. The best dog a person could have.

I turned out the light but didn't feel alone with Star curled up next to me. Then I looked out at the real stars and tried to imagine the old lady's planet. My thoughts then drifted to my treasure box and the things in it.

It took me a while to fall asleep. My chain of thoughts kept disturbing me. Ever since the old woman had told me she was leaving tomorrow, an idea had begun to haunt me. I wished I had never thought of it in the first place, since it would be extremely difficult to make up my mind between two choices. Trying to ignore the thought, I pushed it away so it wouldn't bother me anymore. But each time I opened my eyes and saw the stars shining outside my window, it popped into my mind even stronger than before.

I stretched to reach under my bed and pulled out my treasure box. Spreading the contents out on top of the covers, I stared at them, thinking. I knew that sometime before tomorrow night I'd have to make a choice. I also knew my decision would be absolutely final. There'd be no way to change my mind later.

I felt Star's snout resting on my leg, and I stroked under his ear in the dark. I gazed out at the stars once more and made a wish on the brightest one. I knew it would not come true.

I wished that tomorrow night would never come so I would never have to make up my mind.

CHAPTER TWENTY

Mice in the Meadow

It was just getting light outside as I stirred awake. I hopped into my clothes and crept down the hall to Sassy's room.

"Sassy," I whispered, shaking her. "Wake up."

She groaned and stretched. "What . . . huh?" she mumbled. Her eyes blinked and she let out a yawn.

I lowered my voice to create a sense of urgency. "Get up. I need you to go with me on a secret mission."

"Why?" she asked, suddenly growing very alert. "Is someone trying to steal our treasure?"

I managed to hold back a smile. "No," I said. "Your treasure's safe. It's still in your arm right there." Her arm had turned a pasty, white color, like she hadn't moved it all night. Sassy not move? Hard to believe.

"What mission?" she asked, trying to straighten out her arm.

"If you want to come you can't ask any questions," I warned. "That's the first rule of the mission. Okay?"

"Oh, okay," she said. "Awright, no questions." She vigorously began rubbing her arm. I imagine it must have been tingling badly.

"Your first assignment is to get dressed," I said. "Then come out to the kitchen and we'll eat some cereal so we won't get hungry."

A skeptical look crossed her face. "Did Mom say to?"

I rolled my eyes in mock disgust. "Sassy, how could Mom possibly know about it? It's a SECRET mission. Otherwise, it would be just a PLAIN mission."

"Oh," Sassy said in awe, "a SECRET mission. Should I pack some supplies, like food and tools?"

"Whatever," I said, only half listening. "Bring some stuff if you want. Only we have to hurry."

It wasn't long before we were rolling my bike silently out of the garage. Sassy stood guard, watching for signs of Mick and JayAnn. Then we were off, Sassy riding on the seat behind, me pumping the pedals, and Star jogging along beside us up the street. Sassy was having a great time pretending we were secret spies, her quiet yet constant chatter broken only by occassional commands to Star. Sassy was holding his leash, trying to keep it from getting tangled in the spokes.

Sassy had a bag of who-knows-what sort of supplies that she'd insisted on bringing along. The bag was dangling by its straps from my bike's handlebars. With all of the extra weight, I had to stand up on the pedals and pump with all my might to get a run up the hill. At first, we swerved side to side all over the place. Then, as I gained speed, we started to straighten out.

"What's in the bag?" I asked when we were safely clear of Mick and JayAnn's house.

"A carrot, a dog biscuit, a screwdriver, and Mom's curling iron," Sassy answered proudly.

I wondered what we could possibly do with Mom's curling iron, but I knew it was better not to ask.

"Whe're we going?" asked Sassy.

"To the field,"

"Why?"

"To meet a friend of mine. Hey, wait a minute, didn't I say no questions?"

"Oh, whoops." Sassy put her hand to her mouth apologetically. She could be quiet when she had to. And she wasn't about to risk being left out of a secret mission.

My legs were aching by the time we reached the field. When did Sassy become so heavy? The old woman was there, seated on the rock waiting for us, just as always. But this time she had brought two more cages than usual. I was sure they must be for Sassy. For her part, Sassy stared suspiciously at the old woman.

"Okay, get off now, Sass," I said. "We're going to hide my bike in the bushes until we get back." I unwound Star's leash.

I could tell Sassy was about to ask, "Back from where?" but she must have remembered the no questions rule just in time since her mouth suddenly snapped shut. Then, her eyes shifting once more towards my old friend, Sassy's mouth moved as if to speak, only this time it froze slightly open.

"Come on, Sassy." I reached over, took her hand, and pulled her over in the direction of the old lady. Sassy had grown suddenly shy; she must have expected to see a kid.

Star galloped over to greet the old woman. I had let him off his leash, now that we were safely in the field.

As we neared the old woman, Sassy scrunched up next to me and managed to shield herself behind my legs while still being able to peer out at the old lady.

"This is Sassy," I told the old lady.

The old woman held out a wrinkled hand and gave Sassy a pat on the shoulder. "Hi there, Sassy. I've been wanting to meet you."

The old woman's words and smile made Sassy bolder. "Are you going on the secret mission with us?" she managed to squeak out in an abnormally meek voice. (Once Sassy got used to the old lady, I knew she'd overcome her shyness and become just as hyperactive as ever.)

"Of course she is," I replied before the old woman could answer. "She's the leader. She's the one who tells *us* what to do. You have to follow exactly what she tells you. Can you do that, Sassy?"

Sassy bobbed her head up and down. She was no chicken.

"Are we getting the mice today then?" I asked, turning toward my old friend.

"Yes, the mice," the old woman answered, already seizing two of the cages.

I picked up two of them, and, without even being told, Sassy bent to pick up the last two. I was proud of her. She was not going to be a problem. An expression of serious concentration was written all over her face. Sassy would not fail to carry out her part of the mission.

We traced the old woman's footsteps through the forest. Star kept rushing way ahead of us into the undergrowth, only to come bounding back to join us a moment later. He seemed impatient that we were so slow.

When we reached the meadow, Sassy gazed in wonder. Her face reminded me of how I felt the first time I'd seen it. I could tell she wanted to let loose and run wildly through the grass, but she stood there proudly, even a bit stiffly, awaiting her next command.

"You can relax for now, deary," the old woman said. "Go do what you want for a while. It'll be a fairly long wait, I imagine. Just don't get out of sight."

The four of us spent the next hour or two roaming the field and wading in the stream that twisted through it. Star got soaking wet, and, even though he shook himself from head to toe, carried with him that awful wet-dog smell the rest of the day. Sassy picked a handful of wildflowers to take home to Mom. I had to chuckle at the way little kids pick flowers: some had stems only half an inch long, whereas one was over a foot long, with part of the roots still attached. It made an awfully odd, lopsided bouquet.

"When she says it's time to go, you'll have to leave those behind and quickly grab the cages," I told Sassy, pointing to the sad-looking bunch of flowers in her hand. "We'll pick them up on the way back home. You'll have to keep up, too," I warned. "Don't lose us in the forest."

"I'll run my very, very fastest," Sassy promised, determination coursing through her eyes.

For the next few minutes she practiced dropping the flowers, picking up the cages, and running towards the forest as fast as she could. When she was satisfied that she was quick enough, she went back to her flower-picking.

We sat down in the sun to eat some sandwiches the old woman had brought for us. Now and then, I saw the old woman do the same thing I'd watched her do so often before, only this time I knew exactly what she was doing. She'd squint her eyes as though they hurt, concentrating deeply. I could tell she was sending pictures to the mice, putting images into their minds of what the new planet would be like. How I wished I could see the pictures, too.

Before long, she pointed over toward the edge of the meadow. I could see nothing, but I knew the mice must be there because the grass was wiggling back and forth in places even though there was no wind.

The next thing I knew, we were sprinting across the meadow into the depths of the forest. Sassy ran with true determination and courage. Even when she fell, she scrambled right back up without a whine or a whimper.

When we reached the hole where the first mouse led us, Sassy watched in wonderful delight as, one by one, the mother nudged the babies out. They looked so small and innocent; it made us all smile. When Sassy got to actually hold one of them, I thought she would explode with joy. She held it gently in the palm of her hand, hardly daring to move for fear of squashing it. I'd never seen her be so gentle and patient. All her toys at home had suffered multiple dents, scuffs, cracks, and rips from being thrown around.

One after the other we followed the mother mice until we had collected all of their babies. I felt an overwhelming respect and admiration for the mothers, now that I understood the price they were willing to pay for the happiness of their children. I was glad I knew why the old woman was collecting them. It made it a little easier not to be sad. Sassy, on the other hand, was too young to think much about it. Like most little kids, she accepted things as they happened and enjoyed them to the fullest.

As I reflected on the courage of the mother mice, another thought suddenly popped into my mind, the same one that had haunted me the day before. I still couldn't decide what to do—didn't want to even think about it. Not wanting to ruin my last day with the old woman, I again pushed the bothersome thought deep into the back of my mind.

While we were collecting the mice, Star was unusually well behaved. Not once did he give chase to a mouse or nip at one with his sharp puppy teeth. It was as if all the usual laws of nature were put on hold for a time, subject to a higher law and purpose.

At last the cages were filled. We walked single-file back to the meadow so Sassy could retrieve her flowers. She separated two of them from the bunch and stuffed one through the bars of each of her cages.

"I'm putting them in there so the mice will be happy," she explained.

The old woman flashed her a smile of approval. In a matter of hours, she and Sassy had become fast friends. I have to admit, I was a little envious of how well they were getting along. At the same time, I was glad Sassy was there. Now I had someone else who could share part of my secret. Maybe some day, when she was older, I'd tell her the rest of the story.

Little did I know, I wouldn't be able to tell her until many years had passed.

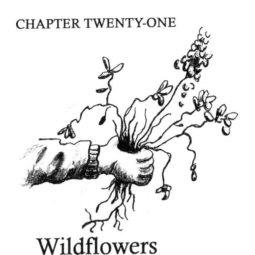

CHAPTER TWENTY-ONE

Wildflowers

U pon reaching the old woman's house, Sassy exclaimed, "Gosh, you don't have very much furniture!" Then she added, "Are you gonna keep ALL these mice as pets?"

I gave her a sharp look and she slapped a hand to her mouth. "Oops, I forgot again. No questions allowed, never, ever."

The way she said it, I could tell she was imitating me. I wondered if I really sounded that stupid when I talked.

The old woman invited us to sit on her back porch and have some cookies and juice. She seemed extra happy, more relaxed than usual. I guess she was relieved to have her work finished. I imagine she must have been thinking about going home.

Sassy, apparently fascinated by the old woman, was exceptionally polite and well-behaved. Perhaps she could sense there was something special, something out of the ordinary about her. The old lady also seemed drawn to Sassy. If I hadn't known better, I would have thought they were lifelong friends.

We bid farewell to our elderly friend and started home for dinner. Holding on to Star's leash and clinging to the back of the seat as I pedaled, Sassy rambled on and on about the mice, the cute way they scurried about, how much they tickled her hands, how fast the old woman could run, all about her house, her garden, and the flowers for Mom . . . on and on . . . and on . . .

When we got home, I had to hear the same old chatter all over again. Mom, who had unusually straight hair, met us at the door. "What did you do today, Sassy? Did you have a good time?"

Sassy opened her mouth as if to speak, then looked over at me. She must have remembered it was a SECRET mission. I nodded as a sign of permission. I knew Mom wouldn't believe most of the stuff Sassy told her, anyway. She was always making up stuff about creatures and monsters living in the backyard and basement. I guess Sassy figured plain old life wasn't exciting enough for her—so she'd have to create her own unique brand of entertainment.

Sassy still clutched the lopsided bouquet of flowers in one hand; the flowers' droopy heads were flopped completely over from lack of water. They were actually dangling below her hand instead of standing upright above it. Of course, Mom made a fuss and pretended to be overjoyed at their loveliness. She tenderly arranged them in a fancy crystal vase filled with water, though both of us knew it was far too late for that.

Sassy stayed right on Mom's heels as she made dinner, prattling on and on about chasing mice and holding them in her own two hands, about the mice giving their babies to a nice old lady, about Star not even chasing or biting any of them because he was such a good dog and she'd trained him so well . . .

I knew Mom was only half listening, but now and then she'd stop Sassy mid-sentence, look at her funny and ask, "You did what?!"

When I came in and sat down at the table, Mom's face wore an unpleasant grimace. She asked me, "You didn't play with mice, did you?"

I certainly couldn't lie to Mom, but I was just as certain that she'd never understand the truth, so I just rolled my eyes and muttered, "You know Sassy."

She never mentioned another word about it. She had heard thousands of Sassy's wild stories. Besides, Mom had her world and we had ours. As long as nothing tragic happened, that's the way things tended to stay.

Mom flipped a stray piece of straight hair back from her face. "By the way," she said, "has anybody seen my curling iron? I can't seem to find it anywhere."

"Yeah," I replied, as if there was nothing weird about it, "Sassy stuck it in a bag and made me hang it on the handlebars of my bike."

This time it was Mom who rolled her eyes.

That evening when Mick and JayAnn came over to play, I spent most of the time off by myself, one arm curled around Star's neck. I still couldn't quite believe he was my very own dog. Yet, it was easy to picture in my mind the two of us doing everything together forever and ever. I massaged the downy fur under his ears until he flopped down and fell asleep in my lap. Holding him made me feel at ease, peaceful.

And I needed comfort, for once again the thought I'd been fighting off all day charged right back into my brain. Again, I battled against it, back and forth, knowing the hour when I'd have to make a decision was growing frightfully near.

For the first time in a long while I was unhappy to see the brightest stars appearing in the sky. Before too long, I'd have to go say good-bye to the old woman, who suddenly seemed like my best friend. Before long, I'd also have to make the hardest decision of my young life.

As we prepared ourselves for bed that night, I promised Sassy that tomorrow we'd go to the forest and feed the rabbits. In turn, she happily announced that we could use the carrot she'd packed in our supply kit. By the time I left her room, she had already fallen asleep, a huge smile stretched across her face.

Before climbing into my own bed, I again took out my treasure box and carefully examined each piece, turning each object over in my hand, still weighing the decision I must soon make. At last I nestled each treasure back into the box, slowly, sadly, as though looking at each for the last time.

As I lay in bed listening for signs that Mom and Dad had settled down for the night, I pondered over the events of the last week or so. Star had nuzzled up beside me. He looked cuddly and innocent, as young animals do. I knew I wouldn't fall asleep, so I didn't even try. Even awake, I tossed and turned, searching for a comfortable position. Every once in a while Star would growl and give me a little kick, probably telling me to hold still so he could get some sleep. For such a little dog, he somehow managed to take up most of the bed. Then, apparently caught up in a dream, his little paws twitched and jerked. I wondered if he was chasing something in his dream.

Before long my mind had wandered, caught up in some commonplace thought, when a clear, vivid image bolted into my brain. For a split second I could see the place as clearly as if I were actually standing there. It was an image of the old woman's house, and I knew it was her way of telling me it was time to come.

Without a second's thought, I jumped to my feet, dressed quickly, and picked up my flashlight. I paused for a moment, deep in thought. Then, I snatched my treasure box, tucked it tightly under my arm, and tied the rope leash on to Star's collar.

Together, the two of us slipped silently out of the house into the uncertain night.

CHAPTER TWENTY-TWO

The Decision

Star and I slowly made our way toward the old woman's house. I still had yet to make a decision. When we arrived, she was waiting at the door. She gestured for us to come inside.

She glanced down at the box pinned against my side. "What have you got there?" she asked. Surely she already knew what it was. What she really wanted to know was why did I have it with me. Come to think of it, she probably had already known the answer to that, too.

"It's my treasure," I said, holding it in my hands. One last time I gazed fondly upon one of my dearest objects. It's brown construction paper exterior had faded through the years; the sides of the shoebox underneath had warped inward—yet to me it was more valuable than a real chest of jewels. I let my breath out slowly in a deep, heavy sigh. Then I handed it to her. It was my gift of friendship. "I'm giving it to you so you can bury it on the new planet," I offered. I hoped she wouldn't think it was a silly idea.

She smiled and took it from me gently—as if it truly was a magnificent box containing the finest treasures. Her words were soft and clearly spoken. "What's a planet without hidden treasure? I believe it's just what the place needs."

I felt relieved. As much as I hated giving up the treasure, I loved the idea of something I owned being out there in space—waiting for me on some distant, unknown planet.

"Will you go straight home?" I asked.

Her weathered features, like the sound of her voice, had taken on a softer, gentler, almost grandmotherly appearance. She flashed an affectionate smile. "No. I'm going to stop off at the new place on the way, leave the mice—and the treasure and flower, of course. You know, I'm very curious to see for myself how things are coming along. Then I'll go home."

By the time the last word had escaped her lips, her eyes sparkled like those of a child. At that moment I could tell how homesick she really was.

We stood there awkwardly for a while, sometimes staring at each other, sometimes purposefully avoiding eye contact. I think neither of us knew how to say good-bye.

"How much longer?" I finally asked.

"Any minute now," she replied.

We waited about fifteen more minutes, neither of us speaking another word. There didn't seem to be anything that was right to say. Besides, sometimes silence says so much more than words. She knew how I was feeling, and I could sense her thoughts, too.

Then, like the unfolding of a miracle, a beacon of light began to form in the corner of the room. My eyes were immediately drawn to it; I could not look away. Mesmerized by its strangeness and beauty, I stared at it in wonder as it slowly increased in size. Soon it had filled the entire room—just as before.

The light was warm and inviting. I began to feel as though I were a part of it, its pulsating energy pouring through me with a great feeling of oneness. My heart seemed to beat in time with each of its vibrations.

Casting my eyes downward, for a moment I did not recognize my own self. My whole body was outlined in a halo of light, a light so peaceful, so good. And, at that moment, I knew I could be anywhere with that light—in the dreariest, darkest cave of a mountain, on the coldest iceberg of Antarctica—and still feel exactly the same way. Enveloped within it, I was invincible.

Seconds later, I heard the same strange humming noise as when I'd peeked through the old woman's window, and I knew the light wasn't the same dead, dull, yellow kind that came from my lamp at home, but a living thing, filled with personality and power. It seemed at once to radiate all good feelings: humor, excitement, tranquility, health, safety, relief, sympathy, belonging . . . love. The pulsating vibrations ran entirely throughout the light—over and over like a heartbeat—and I had a sensation of it hovering above me and under me, buzzing around me and through me. One moment, I'd feel overwhelmed, as though I couldn't stand it any longer; the next minute I'd be reaching out, begging for more. The light had an amazing, overpowering—almost suffocating—presence, but one you would gladly choose to drown in rather than seek to escape.

The mesmerizing vibrations continued to pulsate through it, giving the light a solid, alive, unbreakable appearance. At the same time, it seemed airy, iridescent, and full of color—like a certain type of jellyfish I'd seen in aquariums. Only, it was so much brighter and whiter—more so than even a high-powered searchlight. My eyes were never able to fully adjust to its brightness.

Star sat on my lap, his eyes fixed on the light, completely still and calm—practically hypnotized. I knew he must be feeling exactly as I did.

I looked on as the old woman stepped joyfully into the center of the light as though greeting an old friend. For a split second, I was filled with the overwhelming urge to run to her and beg her to take me along. But I didn't. Somehow I knew it wouldn't be right.

Then something I never would have expected happened. Little by little, all of the oldness about her began melting away. It was as though her skin was a plastic coating or a soft piece of clay. Her wrinkles tightened into fresh, tight skin; her hair, tucked firmly in the tight little bun at the back of her head, grew thick and golden brown, billowing loosely about her face; she stepped out of her plain brown shoes, leaving her feet bare; and last of all, her flowered dress seemed to peel away, revealing a simple, white, robe-like gown underneath that seemed to be made of light itself. She had been completely transformed. And now, not only was she surrounded by light, but it seemed to be coming from her, too.

Under one arm she still gently held my homemade treasure box. The cages of mice rested in a row in front of her. Bending down, she stretched her youthful hand and, one by one, opened each cage. Hordes of little mice scurried out and gathered in a tight circle at her feet. She then picked up my potted pink flower and placed it next to the mice.

I was stunned. There stood my old lady friend in the center of the light, looking like a beautiful twenty-five-year-old. When I say she was beautiful, I don't mean in the movie-star sort of way. Her nose was still a bit hooked, her eyes too close together, her chin slightly thin. But the way she glowed in the light and the look of rapture on her face suddenly made it seem as though a hooked nose, close-set eyes, and a skinny chin were just the very sort of features everyone should have.

Though entirely different in appearance, I could still tell it was really her. I think it was the gray eyes. They had always looked young to me.

"Well, what do you think?" she asked. It was her voice, but a different voice. The scratchiness was gone. It was then I realized that her blunt answers to my questions, which had sometimes sounded cross and cranky, were really just simple language—clear, direct, sincere. It had been the dry, age-ravaged roughness in her voice that had made her seem crabby. Now her style of speaking seemed gentle—really quite elegant.

My eyes followed her every move. "Is it really you?" I asked.

"It's me." She shrugged her shoulders like I'd seen her do so many times before. "The *real* me."

"Why did you always look so old before?"

"I had to," she answered kindly. "I couldn't stand out. You see, when you're around the light long enough, you can't help but have some of it always in you. And when you do, you don't ever want to give it up or lose it. The only thing you can do to hide it is to cover it or disguise it. And I had to keep it hidden. This kind of light doesn't belong in your world yet. People wouldn't understand it. It stands out too much from the ordinary."

She paused and added, "On the other hand, nobody on your planet notices little old ladies wandering around. They can go about their business without anyone taking much interest. I couldn't risk drawing much attention to myself, you know."

True. She certainly would have attracted a lot of attention looking all lit up the way she did now.

A flood of memories washed through my head. I pictured her as I'd first met her, squatting in the field like a child playing in a sand pile. I remembered the trouble I'd had keeping up with her as she whipped through the forest, and how she'd shinny right up the trees to the bird nests. I reflected on how each day she'd always look *too* much the same. Now all of it made sense. I was surprised I hadn't figured it out before. The "old lady" was a sort of disguise, a shield protecting the real person hidden inside until her work was done.

Suddenly, another odd thought hit me. There was a certain part of her that had always seemed old, too. It had something to do with the things she taught me, the way she could make me see things so differently. Looking at her now, she seemed wise beyond her years. I guessed that an average young person on her planet must possess a lot more wisdom than even old ones on ours.

She seemed to be reading my thoughts, for she said, "I'm not as young as you might think. You see, we age differently on my planet—much more slowly. We have none of the suffering and afflictions to wear us out that you have here. When I came here, I took on the appearance of this world, how I would look if I'd been raised here. An age that is considered elderly in your world is, in comparison, quite youthful in ours."

I saw a look of pain pass through her eyes, as though she felt utterly sorry for me. For a moment I sensed she wanted to pull me into the center of the light and take me with her . . . far away from the hardships of this world.

But the moment passed quickly. "Well, this is good-bye," she said. "For now at least. Maybe forever . . . although, something tells me we will surely meet again, sometime, somewhere in this mysterious, vast universe." And then the most beautiful smile parted her youthful lips, and I could tell she was gushing with joy at the idea of returning home. I also noticed she was appearing to fade. The light that encircled her had thickened, collapsing inward around her.

"Good-bye." The word fell quietly from my lips with surprising peace.

Then I suddenly remembered something. "Wait, wait!" I shrieked in panic. "Please come back!"

"You know I have to go," Her voice echoed, as she faded even more—or, should I say, as the light grew thicker around her. "You know I can't stay here forever."

"No, no! It's not that," I cried, fearing it was already too late. I finally had made up my mind. As soon as I'd felt the first rays of light shine on me, I'd known. Trembling, I reached down around Star's neck and untied the rope from his collar. Water flooded my eyes as I gave him a tight squeeze and planted a kiss on the top of his head. He turned and lapped at the drops trickling down my face, trying to lick them away.

Hoisting him from my lap, I held him out towards the lady, trying to be brave. I knew she would read my thoughts and understand. Sure enough, her image grew clear again.

"He's young enough to go, isn't he?" I asked, trying to fight a strong choking sensation as I spoke. "He's just a baby, like the others."

She spoke to me tenderly. "Are you sure you want to do this? He rightfully belongs to you."

"I'm sure," I said, knowing I'd made my decision for his sake, not my own—just as the mother animals had done. The hardest part was knowing I could never change my mind.

She took the pup out of my hands and cradled him lovingly against her chest; my brown treasure box was still braced under her other arm. I looked at her face, then from one of her arms to the other, and realized I was losing my three favorite treasures.

And it was at that moment that I remembered the words the lady had spoken to me the first time I showed her my open treasure box. "Oh, *that* kind of treasure," she had said, "the *best* kind of treasure." Now I knew what she had meant. She was referring to the kind of treasure that's best because it's valuable only to you.

"You know," she said kindly, "if all goes well, you will see him again. I don't know how many years it will be before it all takes place but animals do tend to live significantly longer when the conditions of a planet are better. And, who knows, it could happen quite soon."

I brightened at the thought. I hadn't considered that. "I'll miss him so much until then, though," I said. "Make sure someone takes good care of him."

"You won't miss him," she assured me. "Soon, you won't remember any of this—me, the dog, what you saw through the window, what you're seeing right now. Nor will the mother animals remember. That is the gift they'll be given for their sacrifice."

"I won't remember?" I said in disbelief. "Why did you have me come to the field in the first place if I won't remember?"

"You won't remember it exactly, but it will change you," she answered. "Its effects will still exist somewhere in your mind. The influence of our time together will remain, even though you won't be fully aware of it. It will be the same for the animal mothers. It's best that way. Trust me. You wouldn't go on living a normal life if it were otherwise."

"I won't remember . . ." I whispered the words to myself a bit sadly, but, at the same time slightly relieved. I dreaded the thought of returning home without Star.

She smiled a final farewell. "Still, I'm proud of you. You made your choice even when you thought you'd suffer greatly for it. So did the animal mothers. That's what matters." She looked down at my puppy and added, "And Star will be forever grateful to you."

As she spoke her last words, the light around her again began to thicken, making her appear to fade. Soon, squinting into the brightness, I could barely see her outline—the flowerpot, the mice at her feet, my treasure box, and the fuzzy, faint image of a furry gray dog.

Suddenly, I could no longer bear to look. Turning away, I hid my face in my hands. I could still hear the muffled hum of the light and feel the warmth of its glow on my back and shoulders.

I was totally overwhelmed, and for many different reasons. One day, not long before, I'd walked into a field and my whole life had changed. Later, I'd been given a chance to witness something truly amazing. Then, just minutes ago, I'd lost my two best friends: an old woman—who was now a young one—and my very own dog, the best in the world . . . no, the best in the universe. Finally, just now, at the last moment, I'd learned that I might actually get to see him again. But, most of all, I was overwhelmed by the feel of the light, soaking deeply into me, filling me with a wonderful sensation I'd never known before.

For one tiny moment, I felt like everything in the universe loved me.

CHAPTER-TWENTY THREE

Treasure in the Sky

The warmth of the light gradually faded away. When I knew she was gone, along with my pup and my treasure box, I left the house and wandered over to the field where I'd first met her. Somehow it was the right thing to do. Stretching out on a narrow section of tall grass, I stared up into space, just as I'd done so many times before.

The moonlit night seemed to erase all of the man-made world around me. Stores, houses, telephone poles, and roads suddenly ceased to exist. All that was left was the shadows of trees and mountains, the clouds moving behind them, the large white glow of the moon—and stars, and stars, and stars . . .

I remember thinking, "These are the things that are real, not all that other stuff. These are the things I can count on—the things people can't create and can't destroy."

I think that was the first time I truly understood why the stars were so important to me. As my eyes searched the sky, I wondered exactly where among those bright lights was the place I would go to someday.

Then, something I can't explain happened. As I lay there gazing into space, a strange sensation passed over me. I thought I could feel the movement of the Earth as it turned on its axis. The rotating grew stronger and stronger. Then I felt a hard, quivering vibration pass through the ground beneath me and heard a rumbling noise. A shudder?

A groan . . . a cry for help.

A wave of sadness swept through me as I realized what it was. I marveled that I hadn't heard it before.

Still, I kept staring at the stars . . . for the stars meant hope. Deeper and deeper into space I looked, past the first layer of stars, past the second . . . outward and into eternity. Then, came another sensation of movement. My body seemed to be trailing the path of my eyes, moving out into space at a fantastic speed. The sensation was so powerful that I stretched my arms out to steady myself, clutching the tall grass tightly between my fingers.

At that moment, I knew if I kept looking, kept going deeper and deeper, and did not fear, and did not doubt, I would see it. A wave of excitement flooded my body.

Deeper and deeper my gaze traveled through space, past stars and planets . . . until suddenly it focused on just one. A medium-sized world, green and peaceful, grew larger and larger. Then, for a moment—and only a very short moment—I saw row upon row of newly planted pine tree saplings; I saw baby rabbits and squirrels scampering among them; I saw a tiny gray puppy, still held tenderly in the arms of a young woman robed in white; I saw a brown cardboard box laying in a shallow hole at her feet, and next to it, the tiniest pink flower I had ever seen—so small as to be almost invisible—newly planted in the earth. The woman raised her head as though staring back at me. Her mouth did not move, but echoing through my head I heard the words, "When you look out at the stars, I'll be looking back . . . now, just as always . . ."

That was the last message she sent me.

And then it was over.

My next recollection was a sense of bewilderment, as, glancing around me, I wondered what I was doing lying in the field when I could just as well gaze at the stars from home. Something rough was wedged between my fingers. I looked down at my hand. Why was I holding a piece of rope? Tossing it aside, I felt an empty sensation, as though I'd forgotten something I very much wanted to remember. Struggling to my feet, I stretched skyward.

I didn't know it then, but the day would come when my memory of my remarkable friend, the old woman, would return. At the time, what I did know was that Mom would be rather angry if she knew I was out so late.

On the way home, I remember thinking that maybe tomorrow I'd find Bud and see if he wanted to help me and Sassy feed rabbits.

For information on where to purchase or
how to order additional copies of this book,
please write:

GRAY HOUSE BOOKS
P.O. Box 920142
Snowbird, Utah 84092